Linda Lee Welch is American b... life in England. She is a working musician with her own band, a prize-winning poet, and an associate lecturer in Creative Writing at Sheffield Hallam University. She is currently working on her second novel.

The Leader
of the Swans

Linda Lee Welch

Virago

A *Virago* Book

First published in Great Britain by Virago Press, 2003
This edition published 2004

A CIP catalogue record for this book is available from
the British Library.

ISBN: 1 84408 005 6

Typeset in Janson by M Rules
Printed and bound in Great Britain by
Clays Ltd, St Ives plc

Virago Press
An imprint of
Time Warner Books UK
Brettenham House
Lancaster Place
London WC2E 7EN

www.virago.co.uk

For Nicolhoney

Heart and Soul

My daddy was the one who taught me to sing. Mama taught us plenty of bawdy numbers when we were little and could parrot them without knowing what they meant. *Around her neck she wore a yellow ribbon . . .* I never got the connection between the ribbon and the baby buggy. I only knew her lover was *far, far away.* Tildy thought it was pretty cute, and would stand Bubba and me on the table to perform when she had the officers' wives around for cocktails. I remember one time a very nice lady took me on her knee and helped me plait some modelling clay into a little pot. She was so nice, she told me I was a lovely young lady and I should ignore a lot of what went on around cocktails. I didn't know what she meant, but she made me feel great.

What I really loved were the songs that Daddy sang, and those dark night desert moments when we sang together are some of my happiest memories. His plaintive, juddering voice,

Mama and the boys asleep in the back of the station wagon, just Daddy and me awake and singing the sun up. Sometimes he would reach over and put his hand on my knee, but it didn't bother me.

All the men in my life have come to me through music. Alan and Joe and Gareth were all guitarists. Kevin doesn't play, but he loves to sing. That's how we met; he saw me playing in a pub, and he came over, grinning. 'That takes a lot of balls,' he said.

'Hardly,' I answered. We laughed, and later he came back to my place. Within weeks he was staying most nights. Within months I realized that I'd taken on another soul in need of rescue. But we danced, soppily, crazily, drunkenly, like magic, every night. Until he hit me. We dance less often now.

There is a song playing in my head almost all of the time, a song to fit whatever the occasion is. Music is the duct tape that holds my head together, keeps me from tripping up on the cables. Or, maybe, it keeps me at a slight distance from whatever's going on. My wall of sound.

A Grain of Sand

I was watered and fed at mostly regular and appropriate inter-
vals. I grew through the dry and starved periods without much
damage; I was never swollen bellied or swollen tongued from
neglect. I had a mother, a father, three brothers: perfect bal-
ance. We all still know each other's names and birthdays, and
we sometimes call at Christmas. I have family, for God's sake,
a child of my own now, plus a husband who came and went. A
lot of memories, and a lot of holes. The porosity of everything, finally, is what gets me. Any little thing that happens to
be flowing past at the right moment seeps in without warning,
is contained and held and then slips away again to nestle in
some other crack. And no two people will experience it the
same way, taste or see or feel it the same.

Of course, I believe I've got the most accurate view; I've
made it my business to get to the truth, no matter how hard it
is or what blood has to be spilled. Blood-letting; I prefer to see

it like that. A striving towards health, all our health. At least, we've all lived to tell the tales as we see them. There was a time I thought I wouldn't.

There have been attempts on my life. Not intentional, in some cases, but the death wish was definitely there. I've never wished anyone dead except myself, but I'm over that now. I think I was just trying to help. My parents tried to raise me to be a helpful child.

Tildy, my mom, wasn't aware of my life in the way that I was aware of hers. She knew my faults: *You were born opposite, there was nothing your daddy and I could do about it, you were always a little slut*, that's what she would have said. She never did like me, but then she hardly liked anyone. I was only an exception in the extreme degree of her disgust and her absolute freedom to lavish it on me in a way she couldn't do with strangers. But I am a carrier of my mother, always, of her history and her rage.

There's still a lot I can't quite figure, fuzziness around the edges or plain great holes when I think back. But I'm getting there, and with not a little panache, I've got to say. I'm moving.

Wheeze

Daddy,

You won't want to get this letter. You'll have been sitting in your big soft chair, the one that leans back in three positions, doing a crossword puzzle and picking the bacon out of your teeth. You do look after your teeth. A rattling will sound from the front of the house, signalling the arrival of this morning's mail. This will kind of piss you off. You'll sigh and return to the puzzle, get maybe one more word in place, then put the clipboard down on the table beside you – strewn with ashes and used toothpicks – and stand up. But you won't go straight to the door.

The outdoor thermometer is visible through one of the big back windows, but you'll have to open the curtains some to see it. As you do, the sun will shoot straight in and through the room and make you squint.

When you can see again, you'll check this morning's weather, 97 degrees and rising. Whew. Just the idea of such heat wears you out. You'll wander back to the chair, poking your finger into the soil of all the plants you pass, checking for thirst.

When you get to the chair, you won't sit down. You'll take a cigarette out of your shirt pocket and light it, saying *Oh boy oh boy* as you exhale, shaking your head. Then you'll walk to the kitchen and, stubbing your smoke out in one of the collection of plastic ashtrays on the counter, you'll open the fridge and take out the bottle of iced tea that's always made and ready, turn to the small cupboard by the sink, get a very small glass down and fill it halfway, exactly. You'll drink it standing up.

After putting the tea back and rinsing the glass, you'll lean on the counter for a minute to gather your strength for the thing you need to do next. You'll make your way towards the front door, but slowly. *What's come to me today?* you'll be wondering. *What damn thing now?*

You've got one of those Woolworth's doormats that says ONE NICE PERSON AND ONE OLD GROUCH. Very funny. Doesn't make you smile though. You'll undo the locks and open the door. The heat will be harsh, and even under the protective covering of the veranda, the glare off of the Boswells' Pontiac enough to blind you. Stepping out on to the porch, you'll place your hands on your fleshless hips and look up and then down the road, going through all the neighbours' names in order, wondering how the hell they all are and when you last saw any one of them. Since Mother died you hardly see anyone but your own damn self in the mirror, morning after morning, night after night. Not that Mother was all that sociable; quite the opposite, in fact. But there had seemed a need then to keep up appearances, and you excelled in this task, big teeth gleaming greetings to all passersby. This kept people away from Mother and on the porch or the lawn; the house stayed dim and quiet, apart from the almost inaudible sound of the air conditioning and whatever was on TV.

Thinking about Mother will make you sigh again and shake your head again. You'll turn to go back inside but stop when you catch sight of the mailbox, with its contents visible above the flap. *Oh yeah*, you'll think, and gather the stack to take inside with you. Without even looking you'll know that it's mainly junk mail or requests for charitable donations, plus a bill or two, but Bubba takes care of that now and all you do is just hand the bills to him.

You'll re-enter the house and shut the door, locking up tight behind you. The cool dark atmosphere is a relief and you'll have a little lean on the hall table to readjust and settle into it. Then you'll make your way to the big chair, passing Mother's matching one on the way. It still bears the imprint of her fragile bones, even after a year and other bodies resting there from time to time – the family, the nurses and other caretakers who intrude on your diminishing flesh trying to keep you alive and for what? *Oh boy oh boy*, you'll think and, changing your mind, head for the kitchen table where you'll place the mail. Your coffee cup will be there, a third full, and you'll take it to the microwave for a zap. While it's heating, you'll light a cigarette and listen for the *ding*. You'll take the heated coffee and sit down at the table, thinking, *Am I hungry? I should eat something*. But you're not, and you won't. You'll start looking through the mail instead.

You never did understand the dread that accompanies this effort. For years now just the thought of mail has been troubling. Maybe since the last of the kids left home; just the usual parental concern. Could be that. But that's nearly thirty years ago! No, there's something else, something undone or unsaid, something waiting, and you can't quite put your finger on it. You'll be wondering about this now, as you open the first letter.

Cancer, cystic fibrosis, asthma, crib death, heart disease, leukemia, cerebral palsy; all require your generous concern, and your cash. Bubba says you're a fool, but you always give something to everyone who asks. Well, you can afford to now, and why not? It's good to do something for others less fortunate; it's humanizing. Bubba can go jump in the lake, you'll be thinking with a smirk. But Bubba writes all the cheques now, and you don't want him to think you're a fool. You'll throw that one away.

The next one will be a telephone bill. *Damn it to hell, most people's grown-up children don't call collect*, you'll grumble as you note the amount. *Did ever a man have such useless children as mine?* Bubba's OK, you'll think, *Thank God Bubba's OK*.

Before moving on to the rest, you'll decide you are

hungry after all. You'll stand up and go get one of those
Pecan Sandies you like so well. You'll put it on a napkin
to catch the crumbs, then sit down again before taking
a bite. Looking at the pecans sprinkled on the top will
remind you of the time you made yourself sick, sitting
in a big old pecan tree all day long eating nuts. There
were some wormy ones, and maybe you didn't catch
one or two, swallowed a white worm or just a rotten
nut. You were sick as a dog, green with it, for at least
two days after. It was twenty years before you could
even look at a pecan without blanching. But you love
them now. How you wish you could climb a tree now –
ha! Can't even brush your teeth without stopping to
rest between molars. Kitchen to chair, chair to bed, bed
to kitchen; your life's travels have come to just this.

You'll begin to drift, and forgetting the rest of the
mail you'll drift right over to the big chair and ease
your bony bottom on to the soft leather, leaning back
and breathing out as you close your eyes. A fragile
sleep will descend, not a real sleep, you haven't had a
real sleep for forty years. A stupefying daydream, and
dream you will, for when you jerk awake twenty
minutes later you'll swear you're in Cairo, or is it
Okinawa? And is your plane OK? And who put this
furniture here, Bubba? Somebody's taken all my
furniture and put this awful stuff here! What's going
on? But then, after a few minutes, you'll get your
bearings, light another cigarette, and sigh like the
grandfather coyote you are, no more heart for the
moon. *What a life.*

Oh, Daddy. Life pinches and pokes you enough

without the added discomfort of the unexpected. But you do expect this, have been waiting for years. So you'll go back to the table and sit with your eye on the remaining stack, watching it. No sign of trouble you can see yet, and you're an expert at spotting trouble. All those years in the wild blue yonder did it. Had to have eyes in the back of your head, you said. Used to hang a string from the ceiling of the plane so you could tell if you were right-side up. No fancy automatic piloting then. But you loved the feel of her right under your hands, the vibration rattling your skull, your heart swelling with the total power of it.

You'll be wishing you had even the slightest bit of power now; can't get the front eyes working these days, never mind any others. *Aw hell*, you'll exhale, and pick up the next envelope, adjusting your bifocals. It's *The Retired Officer* magazine. You do like that one, occasionally get to hear about people you once knew. *It's hot in here*, you'll grumble, but really it'll be that discomfort, unease that you never seem to be able to shake. You can hardly tell these days if it's hot or cold you're feeling, but you never feel just right. The air in the house seems to fight you, and the thin film of greasy, clammy sweat sticks fast to your skin. You can't wash it off, any more than you can the past that put you in this present. It just won't go away.

You'll put the magazine to one side, save it for later, and find this letter on top. You'll notice the European stamp and familiar handwriting, and you won't like it, not one little bit. As dread rises in your belly you'll fill your coffee cup, one-third exactly, and then light a

cigarette. *Oh boy*, you'll groan this time, then take the
letter in your hand and slice it open. And out I'll pop,
like the ghost in the machine, the goblin in your
garden. I've come back to haunt you, Daddy, as you
knew I would. As you've haunted me.

Susie

Dream

River, snaky and bright blue, at the bottom of a steep canyon. Village at the top. They need water, but the trip is too dangerous so there is a monthly ritual to pick a young and strong candidate to make the risky journey. The people make a circle of bones and stones and feathers around a big fire. All candidates are dressed in furs belted tightly at the waist with plaited dried umbilical cords. They dance themselves into a frenzy to the chanting of the tribe. The Elder then spins each one around three times. They finish with their backs to the fire, and each throws a small totem over their shoulder on a signal from the crowd. The thrower of the totem that hits the fire first will make the trip down to the river. My totem, a soapstone seal, hits first.

To survive this perilous undertaking, I have to establish contact with the swans. The leader of the swans will help me, but he has to pee into my mouth first. When I reach the canyon floor, he ties me to the bank and creates a golden arc of urine that I open my mouth to receive. It is essential to my survival, he tells me.

I wake up.

RayJan

My life has been a true mixture, from the mundane to the mean to the downright miraculous. This has left me with a lot to think about and plenty of stories to tell, about desert hailstones as big as your fist, three-legged chickens, Uncle Bug's boat, and the day it rained watermelons, just to name a few. So many stories.

One little miracle I'm fond of recalling is the day I met RayJan. It was a sports day or Physical Education event. I remember we were all in gym suits, and different schools had come together to play games. She was on my team for something, four-square maybe. It was hot and sunny and she was the prettiest, nicest girl I'd ever seen. We must have been ten or eleven or twelve, just kids anyway – not a bosom in sight, unselfconscious, you know what I mean. She was so friendly, and she liked me. Everyone liked her, you could tell. She was popular. This was significant, because on that one day, for those few hours, I felt popular too.

Raynelle Janette. Or Raylene Janice. She had a bigger, two-part real name, something southern and fancy and sweet in your mouth. But everybody called her RayJan. *Everybody just calls me RayJan*, she told me, inviting me to be an everybody in her perfect constellation of friends. I couldn't stop twinkling. It was a shiny day. We were fit, and friends, and fully concentrated on moving our bodies gracefully under the California springtime sun. We were good. That's it, I guess. RayJan was good, and in her company I believed myself to be good too.

I suppose there were other things that contributed to the general gloriousness of that day. Mama hadn't had a drink for almost a month, and she was making me a dress. She did still keep a careful count on Daddy's dry Martinis though, glaring across the family room at him with a mouthful of pins as he gradually succumbed to sleep and snoring, at which point she'd chase him out of the room like a bloodhound on a jackrabbit. The twins' braces didn't seem to be killing them quite so much, and Bubba spent increasing amounts of time smoking in the bathroom, delighted with his new skill and sophistication. He could hold it drooping from the corner of his mouth without squinting his eyes now, and his smoke rings were improving daily.

Best of all, Daddy wasn't making so many Hot Italian Sausage Sandwiches during this period. Daddy had a real *thing* about Hot Italian Sausage Sandwiches. Funny, when you think about it, because he was pure *Mayflower* stock, he said. English, Scotch-Irish, with a bit of German and French thrown in along the way. Not a brown eye in the family. Mama was the other way round; the Indians had an edge over the cowboys in her family, Texas Rangers no exception. This was especially evident in her bone structure. Mine too, I guess.

And our big brown eyes. Whenever we visited Mama's mama and daddy and I walked to the Five & Dime for a Coke, people would stop me in the dusty old street and say, *Look at those Indian eyes! You're Tildy's girl, aren't you?* Sometimes they'd even give me a nickel for the Coke.

Even though his blue-eyed blood ran strong, my daddy would get on these Italian Sausage Sandwich kicks from time to time. When he did, he would wake me in the pitch dark and take me into the kitchen, being careful not to disturb the others. It was our secret, he said. I guess he didn't want the family to know he had hidden *Latino* longings. Then we'd go through each step carefully. It was a true art, and being a Young Lady, I had a 'need to know' (he was in the Army). And it was his job to teach me, so he did:

1. Parboil the meat for fifteen minutes: get the water rolling and drop them in gently, so as not to splash. Use tongs if you can find where Mama put them. He would always put his arm around me here and light a cigarette, then start sighing like Aunt Beulah's hound dog Kettle. A kind of whiny groan. *Ten-thirteen-sixteen years of unrelieved melancholy*, Aunt Beulah always said, depending on how old Kettle was at the time of speaking. Poor old dog. It was funny how much Daddy sounded like him.

2. Lift the sausages out, dry on a paper towel, and get the fat in the frying pan hot hot hot. Spit to check. Daddy was a good spitter. He'd practised hard as a boy, and won recess championships regularly. This stood him in good stead for pan-checking. He said girls should never spit, under any circumstances, that I should just flick a drop of water in the fat, being sure to keep my distance, so I did. When the pan spits back, we're ready.

3. Place the meat carefully in the pan, then turn the heat to low. Roll them round good to cover with grease, then cook for twenty minutes more, turning often. Watch them swell and even burst in places, talking back. 'Pure pleasure,' Daddy said through the smoke and spluttering, an odd smile on his face. He loved turning those things, talking to them. It's all in the wrist action, subtle but swift and perfectly timed. He used a long sharp fork for this, which he kept hanging by the stove on a leather thong. He'd had it since he first joined the Service.

4. Fork the sausages out and on to a plate. Get the bread ready to press down hard into the hot fat, soaking up good grease and flavour. No sense wasting good grease.

5. Arrange the fried buns on two plates, open and waiting. Then take the sharpest, pointiest knife you've got and split those hot dogs right down the middle and flatten them out. 'Hot dog!' Daddy always whispered at this time, almost shuddering with the satisfaction of a job well done. Sometimes he'd even cry a little and thank me for helping him, when really, I'd hardly done anything useful at all.

6. Place the Hot Italian Sausages on the bread, sandwich up and dig in. Truth is, they were kind of spicy for me then. I was only little. So I guess Daddy usually ate them both and got me a Coke, or some of Mama's Whitman's Sampler if I promised not to tell her. I kind of think she knew, though. But she never said anything. I tried to bring it up with her once, but she just looked at me with Confederate fury and said, *What Whitman's Sampler?* She'd always acted like it wasn't there, and I guess she was pissed that I knew about it. But we all knew about it, the twins and Bubba and me.

We went through this process whenever Daddy was in the mood, which usually coincided with Mama drinking or one of us four making some sort of grievous trouble. We just couldn't help being troublesome at times, although we did try. It seemed to relax Daddy though, this midnight snacking. I guess he needed it.

Anyhow, that day I met RayJan things were pretty quiet at home, and the sun, just plain old sunshine, made me grin from ear to eyebrow (Mama said I was born crooked, there was nothing they could do to fix it). And then RayJan on top of that – well, I felt great. I was eight or nine, I think. I can't remember which town or school I was in. Maybe ten? Was it California, or Virginia? Not a woman yet, nowhere near, just a kid who figured there might be some hope out there somewhere, and RayJan with her shiny smile and her drawing me into the blissful circle of it just for a day somehow confirmed that for me. She was the sweetest, cutest girl I ever saw, and now when I think about where are cute and nice and sweet and pretty? What happened to them? I think about RayJan, and she's always there, liking me a lot. I can see her right now.

Texas

Tildy was a Texan through and through. Half-cowboy, half-Indian, she had all the skills a girl could ever want or need. She could ride and rope and sing and dance and read and write to beat the band. And she could whistle through her thumbs louder than any boy in Windville.

Texas in 1928 was huge and proud and tough. Since the discovery of oil at Spindletop in 1901, it was getting richer by the minute. Tildy was ten, and the world seemed a promising place.

'Come on, Gracie, let's go!' Tildy hollered at her sister from the bottom of the stairs. It was already six thirty am; in another hour the heat would be murderous. Grace came down buttoning her blouse and holding her sandals under her chin.

'Bye, Mama,' they shouted as they ran out on to the porch and down the steps. Mama was in the kitchen with the baby, making biscuits.

'Keep your shoes on! You never know what might be hidin'
under those big leaves in the shade.'

'We will.'

Tildy and Gracie ran down Park and then cut through Mr
Able's backyard to get to Main. They passed the post office,
where Daddy was already at work, and the Five & Dime, and
Harrison's Photographic Gallery. The dust hadn't risen from
the dew yet, and Main Street was still quiet.

They came to Charleston Road and went left, past Mrs
Etta Grundy's goat Gladys, tied to the front porch as usual.
Mr George Grundy was loading his truck with wood. He was
a carpenter, and his overalls hung down low with the weight of
tools sticking out of every pocket.

'Mornin', girls. Headin' for the melon patch?'

'Yessir, Mr Grundy.'

'Bring one back for Gladys here if you can carry it.'

'OK.'

The land by the river on the edge of Windville town was
communal. Families who wanted to set out vegetable patches.
Most people grew corn, potatoes, onions, squash, beans, but
Tildy's folks spent most of their patch on watermelons. They
provided all the melons for family get-togethers, and there
were plenty of those, what with Tildy's mama being one of
thirteen children and her daddy one of six.

When the melons started to ripen, Tildy and Grace and
their uncle JG, who was just two years older than Tildy, would
get up early most mornings and run to the patch. They'd pick
the ripest one they could find and split it open with a rock,
then scoop out sticky handfuls of the seedless heart of the
fruit and eat it on the spot, leaving trails of juice down their
chins and arms. It was heaven. When they'd had enough,

they'd throw the remains into the river and wash their hands there, then pick another and head home with it.

On this particular September morning, Tildy and Grace arrived breathless at the patch and flung themselves down on the ground. JG was already there. It was going to be a scorcher, that was for sure. Tildy took off her shoes and waved her skirt back and forth to create a breeze, but that just moved the hot air around, so she gave up. She wiggled her toes in the dirt.

'Mama said keep your shoes on, you'll get in trouble,' Gracie said.

'Only if you tell her. Anyway, I'm not afraid of any old snake.' Tildy jumped up and started a wild dance through the big leaves and flowers and fruits. *'Come and get me, snake, come on I dare you! Woo woo woo woo woo!'* Tildy twirled and stomped and flung her arms around. Grace watched her with equal measures of delight and horror. Tildy was so brave.

'See?' Tildy threw herself down by her sister again. 'Still alive, ain't I?'

JG laughed, 'Tildy honey, you never stop trying to show the world you ain't a girl.' He tugged at his white blond cowlick, which served only to make it stand up higher. JG was a good-looking boy. His skin was deep brown from the sun, which made his blond hair seem almost shocking in contrast.

'Mama says don't say ain't cause ain't ain't in the dictionary.'

Tildy was about to reply when she spotted it, a diamond-back, sliding out from under a plant not two feet away. She was transfixed, it was so beautiful, the way it slipped along like a swimmer of earth, effortless. Deadly. Heading straight for Gracie, until it froze. Tildy whispered, *Gracie don't move*, and, never taking her eyes from the rattler, she jumped up and said

'*Yahhhh!*' as loud as she could. The snake slithered away toward the river.

'You're not supposed to do that, Tildy, you're supposed to stay still and make no noise and and and and . . .' Gracie stuttered.

Tildy fell on to JG and they laughed so hard their ribs hurt, they laughed till they had hiccups and could hardly breathe.

'I know it,' she finally gasped. 'I just couldn't help it. I'm a *TEXAN*!'

Tildy picked a blade of weedy grass and stuck it in her mouth, pretending to smoke it like one of her daddy's Lucky Strikes. JG and Gracie followed her example. They lay back in the dirt, smoking, until the sun was level with the courthouse roof. Then they picked a fat watermelon for the family, and a small one for Gladys, and went on home.

Tildy

When Minnie Struck went to Waco to take up a teaching position there, she wasn't aware of how love could steal your heart and turn your mind. She met Chester Clark on her first visit to the dry goods store, accepted an invitation to his mother's house for dinner, and was married in six months. There was all the usual: moonlight on the magnolias, cicadas serenading, the hiss of a rattler as they kissed goodnight. He was the tallest man in town, probably the strongest, and certainly one of the brightest in Texas. He'd made several million dollars in land and cattle deals before dying of bliss at fifty-nine. Miss Minnie didn't feel guilty, just figured we all go some way or other and that way was preferable to most.

Miss Minnie had a sharp eye and a taste for the occult. Her family had been Black Forest Bavarians who settled and named True Liberty, Texas, in the last century. They meant it too; they built and ran the first Women's College in the Southern states, producing a fine line of fiercely bright and independent females, among them Miss Minnie. She turned the running of her late husband's concerns over to her younger sister, Mable, took in lodgers, and set herself up as a medium and clairvoyant – Waco's first. She ditched her corsets and high-buttoned collars and took to wearing spiderweb lace shawls over brightly coloured Mexican dresses. She missed Chester, she did, but with her own mortality that much more pressing, she abandoned both grief and propriety and got on with things. Waco loved her for it.

The lodger business was accidental. Her niece Clara had come to stay for the first six months of Minnie's widowhood, and Minnie found she very much enjoyed the company of younger women. Never having had the good fortune of her own children, she discovered late her innate ability to nurture. So, when Clara left to return to her own affairs, Minnie advertised, and her first guests were Tildy, Bitsy and JimmyLou, three college friends who had just moved to Waco to work. They were operating like a family in no time. Tildy cooked, JimmyLou washed, Bitsy cleaned and swept, and Minnie gave everyone regular glimpses into the spirit world and their futures. Which is how Tildy came to leave Texas.

Bitsy O'Malley and JimmyLou Mason both came from Dallas. Bitsy was a short, red-headed, cuddly girl with dimples and pale blue eyes, and JimmyLou was taller, with brown eyes and hair, and a narrow face with sharpish features. They'd been best friends since grade school and often completed each other's sentences, which could get annoying, but they were lively and full of fun. Bitsy could play the fiddle and sing Irish songs her grandfather had taught her mother, and her mother had taught Bitsy. Her voice was pure and clear, and her vocal range astonishing. JimmyLou (named after her father, James, and her mother, Louise) was a whizz at the Singer; she made her own patterns, and eventually became 'Miss Mason of Dallas', one of Neiman Marcus's biggest selling designers. She would never marry, but would play a big part in the upbringing of Bitsy's eventual five boys.

Tildy Baxter was gregarious and go-get-'em popular with all of her friends. She had an independent streak, and a keen sense of adventure that led her to sneaking into circuses just for the fun of it, or staying in fourth gear in her daddy's Model T, so that every time she hit a bump in the road she'd bounce. She was a great cook; her sweet-potato pie was famous in three counties. She loved to dance, and consumed novels and poetry like candy bars. She read more than anyone she knew, and could recite quotations from Shakespeare and Wordsworth and Dorothy Parker.

Small town Texas was hot and sleepy, and could pretty much tolerate Tildy's whims. She was safe, which wasn't always to her liking, so she sought adventure wherever she could find it.

JimmyLou and Bitsy felt the same. They had all three gotten their college education at Southern Methodist University, where they'd been on the shuffleboard and archery teams together, as well as enjoying the occasional shared cigarette out back of the dormitory. When they finished their studies they all managed to get teaching jobs in Hill County, but with America's entry into World War II, they decided to leave their teaching jobs to support the cause. They got work at the munitions factory in Waco, and they were having a ball. This was a new era for women. No more following in Mama's footsteps; they could wait awhile to breed and brood. They had time and money, and a powerful thirst to spend both. The world had been thrust upon them with what felt like dizzying speed. Berlin, Paris, Tokyo, once pictures in library books, had begun whispering, become possibilities. The exotic was reaching out to them, and they were delighted.

Ouija boards were all the rage among curious young people whose world was up for grabs. The certainties of their parents were water-logged in a thousand foxholes, and this trench-foot of the future led many to seeking consolation in Miss Minnie's front room. Husbands, brothers, cousins were temporarily lost, either in battle or in the US Post Office, and folks wanted answers. Minnie's Teutonic roots stood her in good stead with her customers; they felt her European ancestors might come in handy, even though the Strucks had been in Texas for three generations and had no contact with their Bavarian relations at all. This, combined with her soothing ways, made Miss Minnie's household a bubbling hub of comings and goings. Young women even loosened their collars and started wearing Mexican shawls on the street.

Life was good. They all felt at the centre of something real and intense. Their own boundaries were changing, just as the world's were. The enemy had a face and a name, and would be conquered through unity and will, there was no doubt about that. Of course, the battlegrounds were far away, but that didn't stop them feeling right in the middle of the fray.

Then Tildy's Uncle JG was reported missing in action.

John Gaylord Baxley was the youngest of thirteen children. His daddy had worn out two wives producing them all. Tildy's mother was the oldest Baxley girl, and she'd raised JG like a son. He and Tildy had grown up together, gone to school together, tied lizards to strings and then let them go again, learned to skip and swing and spell and later drive Tildy's daddy's new Model T. Tildy thought her heart would stop. She simply could not imagine her life without JG in it. She had to do something.

After the hubbub had ceased that night and the door was shut, the four sat down around the table, Ouija board between them. The glass indicator sat squarely in the middle of the grainy wooden rectangle, equidistant from YES and NO. The sun smiled in the upper left corner, while a quarter-moon looked thoughtfully across at it from the right. Miss Minnie asked for a joining of hands around the table and said a silent prayer. Tildy's palms were hot and wet. The day's heat still hung in the room like gauze; it had still been 96 degrees at sundown.

At Minnie's nod, Tildy and she placed the tips of their fingers on the glass. *Have we spirit company?* Minnie asked. For ten seconds nothing happened. Then Bitsy, who was impatient by nature, said, *Oh, come on!* The glass started trembling so violently that JimmyLou automatically put a hand out to stop it, but missed as it suddenly swooped to the YES and stood still. *Will you identify yourself please?* Miss Minnie whispered, as if calming a worried child. The women leaned into the table and waited.

MAYBE, the pointer spelled out slowly, AND MAYBE NOT. Miss Minnie had dealt with troublesome spirits before, and settled down for a long slow haul, pulling this one into cooperative mode. It was damn sassy, she suspected. Maybe a child? *All right, as you wish*, Minnie's voice like sugar. *Can I ask another question?* YOU JUST DID, the ghost replied quickly this time, mirthfully, or so it seemed. Tildy giggled nervously, kind of a squeak really. The glass shot round: HAHAHA.

Tildy felt the sweat dripping down from her armpits, curling into the crease under her breast on one side, itchy. She wanted to rub it away, but couldn't take her fingers off the glass. They were stuck there, like taffy to teeth. So she flapped her elbows a couple of times and asked, *Do you know JG Baxley?*, her voice almost inaudible to the others. The glass swooped again to YES, then SO DO YOU. A real joker we got here, thought Minnie, an ectoplasmic comedian.

Is he OK? Tildy's voice wobbled and cracked. The glass started a slow zig-zag between YES and NO, rhythmical, hypnotic; they moved with it as if spellbound, wishing for an answer but terrified of what it might be. A little puff lizard ran down the wall behind Minnie. The house creaked, in warning or pain. The women rocked and swayed like drunken sailors run ashore on sealegs, waiting for the world to stand still. They were a gospel choir heading for the final crescendo and Amen, Amen, Amen.

Then gradually the rhythm slowed, and midway between words the pointer sloped towards the alphabet. TILDY MUST GO, it spelled, then TILDY TILDY TILDY MUST GO. At this the glass circled the board furiously several times before flying up and hanging for some seconds in the air – they all swore to this – then arcing neatly into Minnie's lap. Tildy's fingers were red raw, as if they'd been peeled.

Miss Minnie stood up and put the bright overhead light on. It drove the shadows off and somehow gave the four permission to breathe again. JimmyLou and Bitsy slumped in their seats but Tildy sat rigid, and forward, as if she were already on the journey that would lead her to JG, to Daddy, to grief.

Eileen

Eileen Schatsburger was duped, but she never did figure it out. She just went on believing that she was *meshugena*, that her inability to cope was due to plain orneriness coupled with a lack of proper respect for her long-suffering parents. She broke down, and down, and down again. Things were especially bad immediately following the births of her four children. *Baby Blues*, they called it, shaking their heads. Her poor husband Manny didn't know what to do.

I came across Eileen when I was at college and playing in a kind of Peter, Paul and Susie group, a sugar-sweet hootenanny group, embarrassing now. I had been desperate to be a frail and earnest folksinger, who people would applaud and love and envy for her passion and vulnerability. I borrowed my brother's guitar, a $20 cheapie, and then hung around the folkies, watching and copying and saying very little. I taught myself to fingerpick by repeating the pattern over and over against my thigh during lectures: thumb-one-thumb-two and so on. I threw myself into a relationship with the short dark and handsome Alan and learned badly to emulate his playing, but well enough to get into the band. Or maybe it was the sex that landed me the job, I'm not sure. He'd never done it before and found it wildly exotic that I had. I was an experienced woman in his short-sighted doe eyes, and these were the heady days of *get experienced. In the early mornin' raiiiin* . . . we sang together, thumb-one-thumb-two-ing along. I had a clear role here: to be wistful and sweet. I never got it quite right, but I could feel my face cracking with the effort. I was getting more intensely blank by the day.

We often did gigs at the nearby Army base, which was totally uncool in 1970 but we needed the money so we just didn't tell anybody. On one such occasion I got to talking with the base psychiatrist, Phil Goode, and his wife, Lillian. They'd been to every performance we'd done, and were very friendly. Phil asked me if I'd like to do some volunteer counselling with one of his patients; the military lifestyle was especially hard on marriages, or, more to the point, hard on the wives of soldiers, and his case load was too much for him. I said yes, basically because: 1. I was doing a degree in Psychology and thought I should, even though I was taking 22 credits and working three part-time jobs; and 2. I never had learned how to say no, to anyone, ever. So, I met Eileen, who had already had two of her children, the oldest two, taken into care, and was barely coping with a four-year-old and a babe in arms. I knew nothing about kids, could barely remember being one myself, and realized pretty quickly that this wasn't going to be easy.

I called Eileen, and we arranged to meet weekly in town,

at a diner known for its cheese blintzes, and just chat. I was already on the slippery path to bulimia. It didn't even have a name then, it was just an ancient Greek tradition employed by Jane Fonda and anyone else who wanted satisfaction beyond satiation. It made my eyes swell and my throat hurt, but it had its advantages; eating three pastries at a sitting was one.

Eileen was a thin, dark, nervous woman. She was large boned and angular, and she fluttered and shook like a shag on a rock. She was beautiful, but had no idea that this was the case. Her roughly pinned up hair flew in wisps around her face. She had a wide, sensuous mouth and enormous, distraught and darting black eyes. She kept her handbag clutched in her lap, and leaned slightly forward whenever she spoke, clutching the bag tighter, as if it might suddenly go flying out of her hand. She was thirty-one years old, and like a child.

Eileen had grown up in the Bronx, where her parents, her *ema* and *aba*, still lived. I never did find out what made Eileen as she was. She constantly protested her abiding love for both parents, how good they were to her, and how much she missed them. She was an only child; her mother had lost her uterus shortly after giving birth to Eileen. Eileen clearly felt responsible for this loss. I could guess that this was the root of her problems, but I don't think it was everything.

With Eileen fixated on her mother, and me fixated on cheese blintzes, not a lot of healing took place. Eileen was unable to eat at all: a refusal to nourish herself. What a mess. What an unlikely meeting place. But there we met, for nearly a year. In an odd sort of way, we actually enjoyed each other's company. There was safety inside that diner, inside that hour.

We were polite about taking turns to pay, even though I was the only one to eat anything. We both drank lots of black coffee. We always left a tip.

Our last meeting – neither of us knew it would be our last – was a tearful finale without a farewell. Eileen had suffered a big dip, and would soon be hospitalized, losing all of her children for good. Her husband had found a lover, and she didn't blame him, oh no. What else could he have done, under the circumstances? She'd never been good enough for him, that was the truth. She'd never found *IT* easy. There was something wrong with her, and Manny'd been an angel to put up with her for this long. Her mother always said he was an angel.

Eileen had brought a portable cassette player and was in the process of making a tape to send to her mother, confirming her ema's rightness and vision and asking for nothing, not a stick, not a bean, not a fig. In the tangle of wires, turning the machine on and off, on and off, she cried constantly, trying to avoid sending her sniffles through the microphone. *Ema, this is my friend Susie (sniff off mic). Susie say hi to my ema. Ema, I have a friend, a friend, Ema, this is Susie.*

I simply froze. I couldn't utter a sound, and was thrust into my own occluded despair so suddenly, so vividly; it was the sight I'd been running from for ever without knowing it, the force behind my amnesia, the face behind the lie. *(Sniff) Susie talk to my ema (sniff sniff) please.*

I excused myself and went to the bathroom. I'd eaten two cheese blintzes, which I spewed into the toilet with some difficulty; they were sticky things. Then I cried for thirty minutes without stopping.

When I got back to the table Eileen was gone. I went back

to my dormitory room and called Phil. I told him I wouldn't be able to see Eileen Schatsburger any more due to my heavy timetable. I promised to call him as soon as things lightened up, but I never did.

Seeking JG

Tildy signed up to join the Red Cross, and within three weeks she was in Washington DC for a month of training before going overseas. Minnie, Bitsy and JimmyLou had put her on a bus to Houston, cheering and crying at once, proud of their girl and her courage. Her mama and daddy had driven her to the airport with tears and hugs and hopes that she would find JG. They'd provided pimento cheese sandwiches for the journey, which was by air, from Houston to Fort Myer Army Base in Virginia. None of them knew that passengers were served food on airplanes; none had ever been aboard a plane before. Tildy couldn't eat anything anyway. She was too excited.

The flight was exhilarating. She was flying! She wouldn't leave her seat when she needed to pee; she was too busy watching the sky, being *in* the sky and not under it. Companion to clouds and birds and certain bugs. *I wandered lonely as a cloud . . . Baloney!* Tildy thought. *There are zillions of them, and they're all below me!* She could never feel alone in a world so dense with possibility. When they landed at Fort Myer she very nearly wet her pants.

My mama's generation were united in a war; my generation were united against a war. But the feelings of unity and catharsis were the same. In Tildy's case, Red Cross volunteers were billeted on the Base, where their training took place. Women from all over America shared dormitory-style accommodation and awful Army food. It was the first time away from home for most of them. They were typically single, and bright and adventurous types, so that even though the cultural differences between places like New York City and Boise, Idaho were enormous, they weren't insurmountable. These young women worked hard, and had a great time too. The training was friendly but intense; the girls were intensely friendly, in a way that most probably wouldn't be again. Not Tildy, anyway.

It was her first time out of Texas and Tildy spent every spare minute sightseeing. The Lincoln Memorial made her cry. The Washington Monument literally took her breath away; when she climbed its steps and saw the view she felt her life change for ever. It was a new world, that gave her new eyes to explore it with. She was jittering with curiosity.

Tildy took up with a sweet-faced girl from Boston, and they spent a lot of time together. Judith Mayowitz was a teacher, like Tildy, and a Jew of Polish descent. Tildy had never met a Jew, nor had she paid much attention to rumours of concentration camps full of them.

Judith feared for her Polish relations. She had been born in Massachusetts, and had never met her two aunts or their husbands, or her seven cousins, all of whom lived in Warsaw. But her childhood home had been full of photographs and stories.

Judith felt like she knew them all, and she was anxious about their safety. Her mother, Kristina, had aged visibly in the four years since the German invasion. Their house creaked with moving shadows at night; it seemed that nobody slept.

All this added a new dimension to Tildy's war. The politics of the conflict had never interested her much; it had been just another us and them situation. WE have got to win so THEY don't. Like a high school football game. Talking to Judith was fascinating, and terrible too. Could it be true? Could people really do that to each other? It was almost unthinkable.

Tildy and Judith would stroll along the Potomac in the evenings, or go to Rock Creek Park and wade in the water. Sometimes some of the other girls would come with them, and they'd practise setting splints or making slings out of pieces of their clothing. They would pretend they were on a battlefield, though imagining the actual horror of such a situation was beyond most of them.

One Saturday, about nine of them visited the National Art Gallery. It was June, and red hot weather. They came out melting, and sat on the edge of the big fountain in front of the building. Tildy took off her shoes and stretched her toes. 'Oh, Judy, I will *burn up* out here, I swear.' She eyed the fountain's spray. 'I dare you,' she said.

'I don't think—'

Before Judith knew it Tildy was in the water, her skirt bunched up around her knees, taunting and splashing the others. 'Come on, scaredy cats. Come on!' They all piled in, except for Judith, who sat shaking her head on the fountain's edge.

'We're supposed to be representing our country *at all times*, the Major said.'

'I am representing my country: TEXAS!' Tildy shouted back.

It was later that evening that Tildy received a telegram from Houston. Her daddy had wired to say that JG's remains were on the way to Texas from France. She could come on home now.

Tildy wept, and cursed, and carried on until Judith started to believe it would be a good idea for Tildy to go home. But Tildy finally came around, exhausted, and determined to go wherever they sent her, and the sooner the better. There were only three days of training left. If JG could die for his country, then dammit she could too.

Their postings were announced on the morning after they'd finished the course. Judith would go to England in the first instance, and from there wherever she was needed. Tildy was to be sent to Okinawa, in the South Pacific. They promised to keep in touch, but they never saw each other again.

Officers' Wives

Officers' wives don't work, they volunteer. Officers' wives dress well at all times. Officers' wives will attend church regularly with their families . . . It was like being in school again, and did not suit Tildy's temperament at all.

It had seemed like a good idea at the time. On Okinawa, Tildy had learned to smoke and play poker, among other sophisticated pastimes. The war had been intoxicating, and when she met Walt she was good and ready for that other worldly pursuit, sexual intercourse. He was a Yankee, but she could learn to live with that; it might even add to her new cosmopolitan status. He'd wow 'em in Waco, especially in uniform. After three months they couldn't wait any longer, so they got married in the Base chapel, and Tildy wired the news home.

They moved into married officers' quarters, which were loosely constructed and full of holes. Okinawan rats chewed through everything, even the steel wool used to plug these holes. Walt used to get a kick out of loading his handgun with scatter shot so that when he went rat hunting he looked like an ace marksman.

They danced, they partied, they moved like blind newborn puppies through the heady last months of the war, nuzzling each other for comfort, seeking the security of married love. They lost a baby through miscarriage on Okinawa, but quickly put it behind them. When the time came to quit the island, they went first to Waco, then to Pittsburg. The marriage was proclaimed a success.

'Why, honey, he's just as gorgeous as he can be!' drawled Minnie, and Bitsy, and JimmyLou, and anyone else who got a look at him. Tildy won the hearts of Walt's family with her cute Southern accent and her sweet-potato pie.

Walt decided to stay in the service, mainly because he couldn't decide what else to do. Tildy was pleased; she was adventurous and curious to see some more of the world. But after their third transfer in five years, it was wearing kind of thin, and the rigid code of behaviour was driving her nuts.

Her marriage was a disappointment to her too. Breeding had been successful, and the births of her first two kids had gone smoothly. They had a boy and a girl, just perfect. Walt was a good-looking and popular guy, bright enough, and a reliable provider for his wife and kids. But underneath the surface Tildy couldn't find anything at all. He was like a paper doll, and their brief and infrequent couplings reflected this blankness. He would wander the house at night, then return to bed sighing like an old dog. Tildy thought about leaving him, but couldn't face the scandal and shame of it. So she started ignoring him instead. She refocused her energy and attention on the Officers' Wives Club.

With her tiny waist and her 4B feet, Tildy owned more shoes than she had room for and twice as many belts. She was a lover of accessories; scarves and chains, brooches and hats. Having exactly nothing else to do, she threw herself into fashion. If she had to be well dressed, Goddamnit, she would be. If all she was allowed to do was stand around drinking dry Martinis all day, she'd do it in style.

'Tildy, you should try one of these cute little pecan puffs. Dorothy made them.'

'Just pass me the pitcher, Bonnie. I couldn't eat a thing.'

'Did you hear about General Moberly's goitre? They say it's bad.'

'I'm surprised he hasn't got more than a goitre with a wife like that.'

'They say she's got a nervous disposition.'

'She's just nuts. *Roll me ooover, in the clooover, roll me over lay me down and do it again.* Bubba can sing it the whole way through now. Drives Walt crazy.'

'Oh, Tildy honey, you are wicked! I wouldn't have the nerve.'

'Nerve's all I've got, Bonnie.'

'You've got Walt and the kids, and the prettiest figure on Base.'

'Pass me the pitcher.'

'Bottoms up, Sugar.'

Tildy would return from these afternoons weary and tense. Every day, she'd think, my life is getting away from me a little bit more. She'd try to remember what it had felt like to be thrilled by possibility. She'd conjure up the hiss of a rattler under the porch, watermelon juice dripping down her arms as she rocked in the swing. The heat, like someone's breath on her neck. What had she dreamed of then? What had she hoped her life would be? Not this, certainly not this. Marriage, yes. Children, of course, even if mainly for Mama and Daddy. But not this marriage or these children. This just wasn't right. Only she couldn't put her sturdy little Southern finger on why.

One morning Tildy woke up and went into the bathroom as usual. As she leaned over the sink a rolling nausea hit her and she vomited the entire contents of her belly in one great woosh. *Oh my God*, she thought, *not again*. When had she and Walt coupled last? It must have been a month ago. Had the rubber broken, or what? Tildy couldn't remember. She was usually too drunk to remember much of what went on in the night. Tildy groaned with the thought of a further eight months of this, and then a third child to raise. What she didn't know then was that there were two little lords a-leaping in her uterus, and that soon she would be a mother of four, just like her mother before her.

The pregnancy was terrible. Tildy spent so much time playing solitaire that she saw hearts and clubs in her sleep. She went to the Officers' Wives Club for the first few months, but even the smell of liquor turned her stomach, so she stayed home. Bonnie and some of the others visited occasionally, but she felt so awful it was easier to be alone.

She'd never been sick a day with Bubba or me, or so enormous, so it came as no great shock that she was having twins. At seven months, Tildy looked like a blow-up doll, and she didn't see how her skin could stretch any more. She was urinating so often that she stopped wearing underpants. She could just lift her skirt and squat down quick. Bubba had started school in September, and she surprised herself by missing him. I missed him too, and nagged at Tildy to play with me. I was lonely. But Tildy was exhausted and uncomfortable, and I usually ended up in tears, adding to my mother's frustration.

Tildy had to get up two or three times a night to pee. The twins seemed to use her bladder as a springboard when she was lying down, training up for the big event. It was on one of these weary treks down the hall that Tildy saw Walt coming out of my room. Something was funny about it. His pyjama bottoms were open at the front, and wet. Tildy looked at Walt, at his crotch, then his face, back to his crotch, back to his face, with growing horror. 'What . . .' she started. Then she passed out.

The fall (Walt had failed to catch her) sent Tildy into early labour. When she came round, she was in the Base hospital, having delivered, by Caesarian section, two premature but amazingly robust baby boys. Tildy was woozy with meds and what would become a long-term and raging case of the baby blues. She knew there was something she was supposed to remember, something about that night she fell, but she'd be damned if it would come to her. When Walt brought the kids to see her and their new brothers, what did come to her was a sharp and overwhelming aversion to me, her daughter, her only girl. Tildy didn't know where it had come from, but she knew it was there to stay.

England

When Claire was about three years old, we'd walk back from her nursery up the steep hill to our house. I live in a city built on hills, like Rome, and we were right at the top of one then, while still being only a mile from the centre of town. The city looks as if some giant got a huge handful of houses and factories and churches and roads and pubs and parks, and shook them like dice before letting them tumble down the valleys. A lovely place, but not a lot of planning has gone into it. Not until now, when so much industry has been shut down that the city's planners have had to hop to a whole different tune.

Whenever Claire spotted people through the windows of their houses, sitting alone or together, reading, watching TV, eating, she would say, 'Let's go in and talk to them.' It was hard to explain to her that you just don't do that, invite yourself into people's houses and lives. You have to wait until you're invited, or until circumstances place you together.

I invited myself to England, having no idea what lives I would come across. I arrived in a freezing January, having flown from Seattle to Miami and then on to London. I didn't know what I wanted from this country, but I knew I wanted out of mine for a while. I had a suitcase, full mainly of books, and a guitar, and not much else.

I went to the information desk at the bus station and asked about places to stay. The woman gave me an enormous list, and I picked one in Chelsea, because I'd heard of Chelsea. I got a taxi there. I couldn't believe the streets were so narrow, and so jammed with people. I'd ridden in a bus – 'coach' – from the airport, and several times I'd thought, we're not gonna make this turn or get through this gap, but we did. It seemed only marginally more likely in the cab.

The bed and breakfast was between the King's Road and the river. It was just around the corner from Cheyne Walk, which I'd also heard of. It made me think of Marianne Faithfull and Mick Jagger and candy bars. Here I was, right in the middle of the high life.

I made arrangements with the manager. I would stay until I found a flat to rent, paying week by week. My room was on the ground floor at the back of a large terraced house. It had a pay television and a tiny gas fire, which had to be lit with a match. It was cold and draughty, and suited me fine. It was so *foreign*. But I was the foreigner.

I walked to Piccadilly Circus when I'd unpacked my bag. It was evening now, the shops were shut, except for the tacky tourist kiosks that sold miniatures of everything from Beefeaters to London Bridge, and T-shirts to match. The place was swarming with very drunk men waving what looked like giant green onions around and singing. There were thousands of them; Eros was invisible. I asked someone, *Is it always like this?* She told me that Wales had beaten England at football that day, and the vegetables were leeks. I felt like I was in a scene from a Monty Python movie. *Fetchez la vache!* I kept thinking I heard, but it was in fact Welsh football chants.

I went back to Chelsea in a jet-lag daze and settled in. I was too excited to sleep, so I put a couple of ten-pence coins into the slot and nearly had a fit when the image of a woman's naked breast being kissed by a man came up on the screen. A nude love scene, such as never seen on US television, never ever. I hadn't realized until then that I come from a nation of prudes. I felt myself reddening, even though there was no one else in the room. I watched the film – can't remember what it was called – until the TV ran out of money, then fell asleep, wondering what a leek tastes like.

I jumped up in the morning at the sound of a knock. I couldn't think where I was or who would be knocking, but finally came to and opened the door. There was no one there. I looked both ways, puzzled. Then I smelled something familiar. Bacon. I looked down and there on the floor was a plate. On it were a piece of bacon, what looked like a raw egg, and beans. *Beans!* There was also half of a piece of bread, cut diagonally, that had been fried. My breakfast.

Leeks and breasts, and beans for breakfast. Trying not to get killed when crossing the street: *LOOK RIGHT!* Warm beer and cold houses. *Love* and *Duck* and *Mate* and *Flower*. Cadbury's Creme Eggs. Jumping on buses at the rear. Zebra crossings. I got the hang of it all eventually. I found a flat in Shepherd's Bush, sharing with an Australian woman who was studying *Haute Cuisine* in order to be a better future wife. She was called Breffni, due to her Irish ancestry; her great-grandfather had been transported for stealing a cow in Kilkenny. He'd said in his defence that he just wanted some company, but they sent him anyway.

I got a job playing guitar in a mock-Elizabethan restaurant in the heart of the West End. I was a wandering minstrel, complete with tights and tunic and a hat with an enormous yellow feather sticking out of it. I sang *Greensleeves* ten times a night, part of a bizarre revue put together by Paulie, the jester/MC, who was a rampant queen and a hard drinker. The clientele were mostly tourists, and mostly Australian, German, or American. Paulie's favourite part of the evening was after the yard-of-ale drinking competitions, when he would choose the hunkiest, drunkest Australian man, lock him in the stocks, and take his trousers down. Paulie would then swing from the metal chandelier, waving his hip flask like a trophy over the plastered but appreciative crowd.

The revue included two minstrels, the jester, Henry VIII and Anne Boleyn. I had to be Anne B on her night off and get beheaded, then jump up miraculously and join in a rousing rendition of 'Clang Clang Clang Went the Trolly, Ding Ding Ding Went the Bell', urging the audience to join in with the hand movements. This was the finale, and snatches of several popular songs followed, a curious mish-mash including 'That's Entertainment' and 'Down at the Old Bull and Bush'.

I lasted six weeks in that job. I walked out one night when Paulie was particularly drunk and trying to take my pants down; he'd mistaken me for the other minstrel. I soon found an Italian restaurant, Vito's, that offered me a solo spot five nights a week with spaghetti thrown in. I stayed there until I joined Joe's band about four months later.

What I really loved about London then was the safety of

the city at night. At two am, the doors of the clubs and restau-
rants would open and spill out players from all over the world,
each with his or her guitar or trumpet or saxophone. We
would gather for coffee in Leicester Square, squawking like
magpies over our shiny instruments in their battered cases,
then walk west together, individuals peeling off at Notting
Hill or Holland Park, or, in my case, Shepherd's Bush. We
were a nocturnal community with such a variety of histories
and talents and experiences that it took my breath away. I'd
never known so many different people from so many different
places. I couldn't believe I was among them; I couldn't believe
I belonged among them, but I did.

I got bored playing on my own. I've always preferred to
play with other people, so I auditioned for a couple of bands.
Joe's was the second. The first was a punk outfit called Killjoy,
and I nearly passed out when I saw the diaper pins that pierced
both of the drummer's nipples, a pink one and a blue one. I'm
kind of squeamish like that. They had to sit me down and get
me a glass of water. The drummer, Bear, kindly put a T-shirt
on for the length of my stay, which wasn't long.

Joe looked perfectly normal by comparison. The line-up
was lead guitar, bass, fiddle and drums. They were looking for
a singer/rhythm guitarist, and they chose me. We got along
great, and after two months of rehearsal we made a demo tape
and sent it around. I left Vito's, and we started doing pretty
well for gigs. We called the band *Red Bone Hound*. Joe and I
got closer, and he moved in with me when Breffni went back
to Perth.

We had an agent in Holland, so did a lot of Channel-
crossing by ferry, staying in Amsterdam or The Hague for
usually a few weeks at a time. We played the *jongercentrum*

circuit. They were great fans of our blend of obscure country blues and bluegrass. But going through customs was getting harder each time for me. I had to pass through separate from the band, because I was working illegally. I was being given only thirty days' stay at each crossing, and being quizzed about my money and my intentions. So Joe and I decided to get married. We'd known each other only for nine months, but we got along. So, why not?

We paid five pounds extra so the bans wouldn't have to be called, which meant we could marry immediately. I wore jeans and a velvet jacket; Joe wore the same. Our witnesses were Fiona on fiddle and Jerry on bass. There were no other guests. It was a freezing January day, and we arrived at the registry office covered in snowflakes. The ceremony was over in a matter of minutes; the only words I can remember are 'I do'.

Later that day I called my mother and father to tell them I was married. Daddy wheezed a sigh of relief into the phone. 'Does this mean you'll be staying in England?' I was off his hands, he thought. I told him yes, for now anyway. Tildy said only, 'Good luck to him; he'll need it.' I hung up, wishing I hadn't called.

Flying

Tildy jumped prettily from the cockpit of the Aeronca F-65, feeling on top of the world. She'd done spins, spirals, stalls and a forced landing. She'd just completed her ninth solo flight, and would have her pilot's licence in six months if everything went according to plan. Just wait till they heard back in Houston.

Walt wasn't so sure about women flying, but Tildy was headstrong; nobody in her life had ever denied her anything she wanted, and she wasn't going to start giving in to a mere husband. So there.

As she headed for her Jeep, Tildy noticed again how sore her bosoms were, swollen and tender. She had only spotted during her last period, and she was a week overdue for another one now. They'd been using rubbers, so it couldn't be . . . could it? She was only just beginning to understand the ins and outs of the whole business, as it were. But she was pretty sure she couldn't be pregnant. Walt was adamant about their first child being born on American soil.

She hopped into the driver's seat and suddenly bent double with cramp. She held her belly tight and moaned and felt the blood start pouring out between her legs. It spread over the seat, wrapping her in its heat and stench. Tildy passed out.

She came to in the Base hospital, a nurse changing the drip stuck in her hand. *You lost a lot of blood*, she said softly. *Try and rest.*

What happened? Where's Walt?

He's just gone out for a cigarette. You miscarried. You were two months pregnant. Your husband told me you didn't know. I'm sorry.

Tildy could hardly take it in. *Pregnant?*

You have plenty of time to try again. It's very common, often something wrong with the foetus.

Tildy thought of her Aunt Beulah, nine miscarriages and the closest she ever got to a child was her hound dog Kettle. Dear God, she thought, and closed her eyes, I don't think I could take it.

Walt came in and sat on the edge of the bed. *How ya doin'*, *sweetheart?* He kissed her forehead.

Tildy took his hand and put it to her eyes and cried into it. *It's OK, Tildy. It's OK, hon. But no more flying. The doctor says it's not a good idea.*

Tildy froze. She let go of Walt's hand. *Why?*

Better safe than sorry. You know. Anyway, there's only going to be one pilot in this family, and that's that.

Tildy turned her face to the wall.

I'm gonna grab a bite to eat. I'll be back in an hour or so. OK, hon? Tildy?

Tildy groaned, and shut her eyes. Walt fairly strutted out of the room. He wasn't worried. He was fertile, they were young, and now he had his wife on the ground where she belonged. It felt right.

A kernel of bitterness planted itself in Tildy's heroic and unsuspecting heart and took firm root. And that was that.

Taco Tia

I really hate graham crackers. This aversion has been with me since we lived in Riverside, on the edge of the Mohave Desert in Southern California, surrounded by orange groves. It was 116 degrees in the shade most of the time, but the winters could turn frosty. There were smudgepots to protect the oranges from frost. You only had to touch your cheek when the smudgepot fires were going to leave a black streak.

Riverside was tough on Tildy. We lived in a neighbourhood with few children, mostly elderly, retired folks who kept themselves to themselves. Daddy was flying a lot, away for months at a time, and Tildy took advantage of this lack of scrutiny. She drank and passed out and woke up and drank again. Bubba did his best to keep things together. He searched the house for gin and poured it down the sink, which made Tildy positively luminous with rage. *Goddamnit to hell, what are you DOING, Bubba?* She'd pound her fist on the kitchen counter, rattling the pots and pans. He hid the car keys so she couldn't drive to get more, but she drank anything she could find: perfume and aftershave, food flavourings, Listerine. She had determination, and it worked.

Bubba got us to school and usually managed to find food. Tildy hid her wallet, but he would get us looking in the bottoms and zipper pockets of all her handbags for loose change – she had a handbag to match every pair of shoes she possessed – and he had weekly money from his newspaper round. We were a sad little crocodile, winding our way down the hill to the Taco Tia, Bubba in the lead. We'd count our pennies out on the counter and buy as many 19 cent tacos as we could afford, then sit in a booth together, eating them, with grease and hot sauce running down our arms and chins. Funny, but this is a good memory, of smell and taste and being together, of watching the streetlights winking on, twinkling in the warm California night.

We never knew what we'd find on our return from school; Tildy passed out in a heap, girdle round her ankles and covered in puke, or Tildy just drunk enough to be really nasty, tossing insults like grenades at whoever got too close. This isolated us even further, because we could never invite friends home. I tried it once, when Daddy was away somewhere. I entered the house with my friend Katy to find Tildy curled like a rattler in her chair. *Who in the hell are you?* she hissed. Katy was cool about it. We just went outside to play. But she never came again.

So, Bubba, the twins and I were thrown on each other in a way that still has repercussions now. We spent (except for Bubba) too much time in tears. Bubba kept his chin up, his shoulders squared, and his little boy's hands in fists.

There were periods when Tildy was OK, when Daddy was

around and she would direct her considerable energies into projects: writing a school newspaper, developing her skills as a dressmaker, studying the Bible. Mama had more books on the Bible than anybody I've ever seen. But I have no idea how she saw her spiritual self, how all this studying influenced her world view. I guess she believed in heaven; I wonder if she figured she'd make it there. When she was good, she was very very good; this must count for something.

It was in Riverside that I spent a lot of my time perfecting my spinning technique on the playground bars. I always wore shorts under my skirt so I could climb up, hook one knee over, and, grasping the bar on either side of me, spin like crazy, around and around and around, without showing my undies. I spent every recess and hours after school practising. I could spin better and faster and more times round than any other girl in my class, and it brought me respect, with one exception.

Geena Maxwell was one of the few other kids who lived in my neighbourhood. She was a strange girl with an even stranger family. Her sister was called Clarabelle, which I thought was hilarious, considering Howdy Doody's cow and all. They were always stroking each other, Geena and her sister and mom and dad. Like they couldn't stand to be out of each other's sight. They were a very tight unit, and a very odd unit too. Geena was about my height and size, wiry and strong, but the others had a slightly lumpen look about them, and enormous feet. I sometimes wonder if Geena's feet ever reached the family proportions, and if there was some kind of penalty if they didn't. Maybe her family disowned her at eighteen for her 4Bs, or made her hide her bottom half in family photographs; I don't know.

Geena and I had walked to school together a few times, the twins and Bubba running on ahead. But she was increasingly annoyed with my growing stature in the playground, and so started hanging around and then following a few steps behind me on the way home from school, taunting and teasing and calling me names. *Susie's just an ugly ugly girl. Stupid Susie, Susie Stupid. You wanna fight me, Susie Spitball? You wanna fight? Stick 'em up, Susie Stupid. I dare ya.*

She kept this up for days. I stayed later and later in the playground, spinning until I was dizzy from it, but Geena was always there, lying in wait. She wouldn't have dared with Bubba around, so I was safe in the morning. But the afternoons were getting worse. I tried to just ignore her; I was useless in confrontations and never knew how to answer back. *Gonna getcha, Susie Cream Cheese. You better watch out . . .* and I'd just hang my head and speed up my step, hoping she'd go away. But the day came when she was so frustrated by my inability to rise to her bait that she pushed me and I fell, bloodying both knees and spilling hot tears all down my face. *LEAVE ME ALONE!* I screamed at her, *JUST LEAVE ME ALONE!*

We were near my house when this happened, and Tildy was in good shape at the time. She heard me shouting and came out of the front door with a mop in one hand and a cigarette in the other. *What's going on?* she barked, and Geena and I both froze. Tildy took a look at my knees, and at Geena's satisfied gloves-up stance. I lost it then. I sobbed, *She follows me and calls me names and she pushed me down and she won't leave me alone.* I scrambled to my feet and stumbled up the steps to our front porch. Tildy put her arm around my shoulders and narrowed her eyes at Geena, who was looking less dangerous by the minute.

If I ever catch you bothering my Susie again I'll tan your hide and tan it good. Do you understand me? Tildy shook her mop in Geena's direction. *An eye for a Goddamned eye. And you can tell your mother I mean it, too.* She squashed her cigarette out with a neat twist of her toe and bundled me into the house. I could hear Geena sniffling as she turned to run home. Tildy took me into the bathroom and washed my grazes, then sat me at the kitchen table and gave me some cookies, even though it was nearly dinnertime. I ate them while my mother chopped vegetables, an onion, a pepper, tomatoes. The smoke from her perpetual cigarette swirled round the room in slow motion. We didn't speak. I held my breath; I didn't want this moment to end.

Geena never bothered me again. Daddy left for Turkey the following week and Tildy went on a big one. We ate nothing but graham crackers for six days, at first with a layer of jam sandwiched between two, then plain, when the jam ran out. Then Bubba got some birthday money in the mail – he turned nine – so we were all right. No more graham crackers, not ever again.

The Twins

The twins came bawling into the world with such force and fury that everyone stood back amazed. This was unheard of in C-section babies; they were usually doped up and placid for at least a few days, not screaming the place down like Franklin and Frederick, or Brother and T'other, as they were called. This rage would stay with them all their lives. They would never marry, but live together, working furiously at the same job and smoking angrily the same cigarettes.

Tildy couldn't cope, even with help. Her hormones were all over the place and her stitches itched like hell. At least she could drink again, which was a relief. Gin had made her retch during pregnancy, so she'd laid off it. Now, it felt like a dry Martini was the only good friend she had, her only source of peace.

Bubba and I were alarmed by our brothers' behaviour, and tended to keep our distance. Bubba was loving school, and I had learned how to be solitary, amusing myself with books and crayons. I was obsessed with American Indians and spent weeks trying to make a wikkiup in the backyard. But, as Tildy foundered, I was increasingly called on to help the nanny with Brother and T'other. I grew fonder of them, just as Tildy was withdrawing further and further from all of her children, until finally the cutting off was complete.

Bubba and I were left with a longing, a grief, a memory we couldn't quite grasp, while the twins couldn't miss something they'd never experienced, so they just got more furious. We all felt out in the cold, except for our father's odd bursts of affection, usually when he was drunk.

Frank and Fred were identical twins all right, but in many ways they were complete opposites. Frank did all the talking, while Fred was mostly mute. Fred was an outstanding athlete, even though neither of the boys grew beyond five feet four inches. He played on all the first teams in school – football, basketball (he could really jump) and baseball. He became something of a hero in high school due to scoring so many goals and taking the Wilson Wolves to the top of the Schools Football League for the first time in the school's history. Frank was ball boy or general stepandfetchit for every team Fred was in, and provided a running commentary on each game to whomever would listen.

Both boys were bright, but not particularly inclined to academic pursuits. They loved the outdoors, and were ace shooters with their twenty-twos, bought for them by Daddy on their twelfth birthday. They amassed so enormous a collection of squirrel and gopher tails that it required a separate crate each time Daddy got transferred and we had to move. In between moves, the trophies hung on their bedroom walls, giving the room a musty, bloody smell, which they loved.

They didn't have close friends; neither saw the need. They had depended on Bubba and me for as long as it was necessary, and loved us as well as they could. But all they really required was each other. When they finished high school, they hit the road, and ended up in Greensboro, North Carolina, where they got portering jobs at the hospital. None of their colleagues could tell them apart, so they were both called Twinnie by anyone who wanted them. They bought a small house outside of town and spent their spare time hunting and fishing, depending on the season.

This was the most serene their lives had ever been, so they didn't like it one bit when I wrote to them, asking if they remembered anything funny going on when we were little. I wrote:

Hey, guys,

How are you doing? Catch any big ones lately? Hope so. Claire's almost FOURTEEN now, would you believe it? She gets smarter every day. I'm sending a picture so you'll know she's taller than I am!!! It ought to be against the law for kids to outgrow their mothers.

Joe is still at the university, and I'm thinking of going back to college to get some sort of qualification. Haven't decided what yet – depends on who'll have me!

I want to ask you guys something. I've been having some funny pictures popping up in my mind recently. Old memories. It's been pretty weird. Memories from way back, mostly to do with Daddy. God this is hard to write . . .

I think Daddy messed with me. No, I KNOW he
did. I KNOW IT. I just wondered if you guys
remember anything about it. Anything at all. It doesn't
matter if you don't. I just wanted to ask, that's all. If
you were aware of anything funny going on.

Must be deer season coming up. Are you still using
bows and arrows, or have you converted to Carolinan
muskets?

Take care, and please write back.

Love, Susie

The old fury welled up, and they did write back, immediately:

The only funny thing we can remember is you. You
were always crazy, Susie, everyone knew that.
Remember when Mama had to take you to the doctor
you were so nuts? And every other night Bubba or one
of us had to drag you out of the shower where you
were scrubbing your skin off in your sleep. THAT'S
funny, Susie. Not Daddy.

Just get on with your life. There's no point digging
up dirt, it'll only hurt you. We'll call you at Christmas.

It was a minor disturbance, and after a week had passed they
had probably forgotten all about it. At least for the time being.

Korea

Walt was in Korea for a year. When Tildy heard about this posting, she packed up the kids and moved to Houston. She was bored with the military life, and thought if she had to talk to another officer's wife she'd end up spitting right in her face. Not that she didn't like or identify with these women, just that their collective frustration and attempts to hide it led to hard-boiled banalities that Tildy was losing the ability to stomach. Texas would ground her. She wanted to lay off the gin for a while too.

She got to see a lot of JimmyLou and Bitsy that year, and Miss Minnie too. JimmyLou came to Houston the most. Her dress-making business was already flourishing, and she'd taken on staff to free her time up some.

One hot Friday afternoon in late May, Tildy and JimmyLou were sitting on the back porch of Tildy's rented house, drinking Martinis. Bubba was in school, the twins were taking a nap, and Susie was swinging on the swing set in the backyard. The rhythmic creaking of metal on metal punctuated the sultry air.

'I like it better when he's not here.' Tildy ran her hand through her wavy and wayward mop of hair.

'You can't say that, honey!' JimmyLou was positively unnerved. 'You shouldn't even *think* that. Why—'

'I know it, Goddamnit. But it's true.'

JimmyLou sipped her drink slowly. 'You've got to do your duty, Tildy. You've got four children. They need their daddy.'

Tildy laughed bitterly. 'My duty? I've done my duty to God and creation, Jimmy. I bore four howling infants into this world. I feed and clothe them, I clean up their messes. But my own mess I can't get free of. There's something . . .'

'What, sugar? What is it?'

'Walt. He's like tapioca pudding. I can't find a solid centre, it's like leaning on mush.'

'Now, Tildy, I never would have taken you for wanting to lean on anybody.'

'That's not it,' Tildy sighed and downed her drink, reaching for the jug at the same time. She refilled her glass, and offered the same to JimmyLou, who declined. The women were watching Susie swinging higher and higher. The child had a cast on her right arm, but it wasn't stopping her.

'How'd she break her arm?' Jimmy asked.

'That child is always doing herself some mischief or other,' Tildy answered. 'She was showing off, as usual, shimmying up doorframes like a monkey. It was at Mother's. She missed her grip and landed on her wrist. Took Doc Brewster two hours to set it, the break was so clean.'

'When's the cast coming off?'

'Next week, thank God. Then she can go swimming with the others. I can't stand that child in my hair. She drives me crazy.'

JimmyLou smoothed her skirt as she stood, and leaned on the porch railing. 'What are you going to do?'

There was a long pause. The cicadas were making an almighty racket. 'Nothing.' Tildy held her glass high and shook it so the ice cubes tinkled. 'Not a Goddamn thing.' She drained it dry and poured another.

'Well, sometimes—'

'You don't have to tell me, Jimmy. Do you think I could do that to my mother and daddy? Oh, God,' she groaned. 'Some days I wish they'd just lock me up.'

'Don't say that, sugar.' JimmyLou's voice was sharp. 'Don't ever say that.'

Tildy looked at her friend, her beautiful and talented and fancy-free friend and wanted to weep. 'All right,' she whispered, lighting a cigarette. She felt her life drifting away from her like so much smoke, stretching and thinning until there was nothing there at all.

JimmyLou turned back to Susie on the swing. The girl looked like she would fly off to Kingdom Come, or wrap herself so hard and fast around the bars she'd get crushed.

'Isn't she swinging a little too hard on that thing?'

Tildy eyed her daughter for a minute, shaking her head. Then she spoke. 'Yes, that's the truth.' She stood up and gathered the jug and glasses in her hands. 'Let's go inside.' Tildy opened the screen door and JimmyLou followed her into the kitchen. Susie didn't notice.

Cramp

I was in pain. It was the summer vacation, and most days Tildy drove us to the swimming pool, where we swam and ate french fries in between swims. We could also sign out chess-boards and pieces, or checkers, so we played games and sunned ourselves all day, and were well entertained and out of Tildy's hair.

On this day I had a terrible cramp in my belly. I lay curled up on my bed, crying. Tildy was furious with me; she was certain that all I needed was food. I refused to eat a bite, until Tildy forced a tuna fish sandwich into my mouth and made me chew and swallow.

I realized that I was starving. I should have known; Mama was always right. I ate the whole sandwich and asked for another one. Tildy was enraged by this point. *You've spoiled everything. Bubba and the twins wanted to go swimming but it's too late now. How the hell could you forget to eat? What the hell is the matter with you?*

Mama, please, I'm sorry, it's not too late, it's only two o'clock, Mama, please, I'm sorry.

Tildy growled, but relented. *Get your things then. Hurry!*

The pool was crowded when we got there. Bubba and the twins and I stuck together, with Bubba in charge. But I was always the last one out of the pool when they blew the whistle at five o'clock. I was a seal in the water, sleek and perfect, quick and strong. I was at home in the water like nowhere else, my whiskers gleaming and my flippers flipping. I could swim two lengths underwater, both diving in and pushing off the wall.

I stood at the edge of the pool and waited for a space to dive into. I loved that feeling, my body slicing into the blue, the chill of it, the chlorine and the bubbles as I breathed slowly out of my mouth, the ease with which I squinted and snaked my way around legs and torsos to get to the deep end, as deep as I could go. There I let my body hang in the water's arms. It was the only time I could really relax. The rest of life required vigilance; here, I could suspend my watch. The lifeguards worried at first, were forever blowing their whistles or diving in to save me, I could stay under so long. But they got to know me, and left me alone. I was a seal.

Scrabble

Joe was an eccentric character, I knew that right from the start. He was long and lean, with a broad forehead and big blue eyes. His cheeks bore the scars of teenage acne, which he attempted to hide with lambchop sideburns, and occasionally a beard. His interests ranged from bird watching to long-distance running to serial killers to obscure science fiction from the forties and fifties. Olaf Stapleton was top of the list, followed closely by Simak. Joe's was an obsessive but somehow cartoonish world. *Zap* was his favourite word, and he said it a lot, even to himself, under his breath, as he cooked dinner or changed the strings on his guitar. He was like a buzz-saw on a distant hill, a low-level hum. *Zzzzap* . . . as the onions hit the oil. *Zzzzzzzap* . . . as he wound his E string tighter.

He was estranged from his parents, but wouldn't discuss it; I never met them, and never did find out why. But, apart from occasional periods when he was convinced he was being controlled by aliens – *They're watching, Susie. They're here* – he was a solid, bright and loving partner.

We'd settled down and Joe had gotten a day job. I loved being pregnant. I was contented and full of energy and so horny I wouldn't leave Joe alone. He'd race home during his lunch hour and I'd be unbuttoning his jeans before the door was shut behind him. Life felt enhanced; I was taking part in a small miracle.

We were playing Scrabble with our neighbours when my waters broke. I stood up with a bowl of popcorn in my hand and *gush*, all down my legs. I wasn't having contractions yet, but all the same Joe raced down the road to the phone booth to call an ambulance. We didn't have car or phone in those days; life was simple.

The ambulance came. We had chosen a low-tech delivery, so we were taken to a small nursing home on the outskirts of town. We settled in for the delivery, me in bed and Joe sitting in a chair beside me. The next thing we knew it was morning, still no contractions and Joe cramped from his uncomfortable sleep.

The bullish matron came in and told us we'd have to go to the big hospital and have the labour induced. We protested. We'd studied up on induced childbirth and wanted none of it. The matron told us we were fools and stormed out. A sympathetic nurse suggested we take a jog around the grounds; this might get things started. We did, but it didn't.

When we returned from our run they were all out looking for us, as if we were escaped convicts. A doctor from our practice was there, one we didn't know. We were ushered into our room and hollered at: *I've been warned about you, all this hippy philosophy, you're going to have to—*

I lost it completely then, screaming, *I don't even know you!*
The doctor stopped, said sorry, introduced herself, and
explained that once the waters have broken there's a risk of
infection. No one had told us this, and it was one eventuality
that we hadn't researched. We said OK, we'll go, of course
we'll go.

We were escorted to the hospital by the manager of the
nursing home, in an ambulance. I guess they thought we'd try
and make a break for it, go and squat down in the woods
somewhere. Nowadays, all that we asked for is considered
common practice. But back in 1977 they said we were nuts.

Even with the induction, the labour was a perfect eight
hours, and I, the biggest coward I know, managed it without
painkillers, even gas and air. The second stage was only fifteen
minutes, and the student midwife, who'd gone for a break,
nearly missed her 'catch'. When the baby came out she
crawled up on to my breast and sucked. It was the most excit-
ing thing that's ever happened to me, as if the sky had opened
up to reveal the heart of the whole shebang.

Oh, it's a girl, by the way, the midwife said. Sister Pride was
her name.

We know, we startled ourselves by answering. We hadn't
looked, but we must have always known. *Claire. Claro. Clear.
Claire.* It had taken some effort, but we'd managed something
beautiful between us. Something good and strong and lasting.
We thought.

The Scissors

It was bad. Even in her nauseous, fuzzed-up, shaky state, Tildy knew it was pretty bad. Daddy had been gone three? four weeks, and she hadn't been fully conscious for one day of it, except maybe the first few hours. Now he was coming home, and she wanted to avoid a major scene, so she was making herself some coffee. The gin was gone, the bourbon, the beer, the Listerine, plus every bottle of aftershave that Daddy had possessed. She felt pretty awful, but coffee would help.

Tildy filled the kettle carefully and put it on the burner to boil. Luckily they'd just acquired one of these new fancy electric stoves; she was sure she couldn't have struck a match if you paid her. She leaned against the draining board and tried to breathe. The kids were here somewhere, she guessed; was it a school day? What time was it? *Oh God*, she moaned, *those kids'll be the death of me yet.*

The next thing Tildy knew, a shrill screeching whistle

penetrated her skull. She cringed and blindly grabbed for the kettle, but picked it up too close to the metal and in a white-hot second both Tildy and the boiling water were all over the floor. Her mouth was bleeding badly and she must have screamed or groaned or rattled, because Bubba, the twins and I were staring big-eyed at the kitchen door. Tildy's insides lurched. She struggled to sit up, hanging on to the drawer handles, but fell back with a bang on the hard cold linoleum.

Tildy came to, sitting up in bed with Bubba leaning over her pressing an old washrag against her mouth. She gagged and pushed him away as hard as she could. He didn't lose his footing much, just stepped back really, holding the bloody cloth in his hand and gawping at her. Something felt very wrong.

Bring me a mirror, she rasped. I got the vanity glass from Tildy's dressing table, which was overflowing with perfumes, bobby pins, nail files, empty glasses and cigarette ash. I handed it to my mother, who held it shakily up to her face. What she saw was not the full scarlet mouth of the Southern belle she was born to be, but about half of a bloody top lip hanging by a sliver of skin down to her chin.

Give me those scissors, she barked as well as she could manage under the circumstances, pointing to the manicure set on her dresser. We were horrified. The twins and I cowered behind Bubba, and waited.

No, Bubba whispered.

What?

No, said Bubba again, but with more conviction.

Give me those Goddamn scissors now!

Bubba had never disobeyed his mother once in his ten years. He wasn't sure he could do it.

Susie, give me those scissors.

I just stood there, looking from Tildy to Bubba.

Bubba said, in a desperately friendly tone, *If you cut your lip off you won't have a lip any more, Mom. I'll get you a Band-aid.* He turned and went to the bathroom. Tildy just scowled at us until Bubba came back, tearing the paper wrapper off of the Band-aid and peeling the strips off the sticky bits. He hesitated at the bedside.

Let me stick it on for you, OK, Mom?

Tildy grunted and gave up. She leaned her head back on the pillow, disgusted with everything now. Even her kids were turning against her. Bubba put the Band-aid on carefully, trying to get the lip back in its proper place. Tildy winced, but didn't interfere. What was the use?

Now get out of here, she mumbled with some difficulty. And we did.

Daddy came home later and was mad at everyone. *Damn it to hell, damn it to hell,* he kept muttering under his breath, and pouring large Martinis, very dry, in order to cope.

Wheeze II

. . . Sit comfortably, Daddy. I know your back hurts all the time, and the brace rubs your withered flesh raw, so you usually leave it off until the nurse catches you. I can feel your pain, Daddy, I really can. So, sit up as straight as you can, lean into the soft green plastic cushioning on the back of your kitchen chair, and try to relax. I want to talk to you.

How did it affect you, growing up the son of an undertaker? You described it with great humour, collecting corpses with your father from the age of seven; always said it was only bad if they weren't in one piece, or if they'd been left so long they smelled. You told me you first drove at ten years old, and it was the 'dead wagon', complete with a body in the back. And all the time my grandfather lived unbearably surrounded by the cornfields he wished were his own.

He longed for a farm, but land was expensive and he was lucky to even have a job. A man had to make do, and he did, but his frustration and longing led to moods his children watched for and tried to avoid.

Did this perpetual rounding up of the dead and gone leave its mark? An emptiness, a reduction of sensation or of hope? I can imagine it did. But you triumphed. You shone in school and went on to fly airplanes, becoming the handsomest do-or-die Prince of the Sky the Army ever saw, a silver-winged hero, a boozin' buddy. You never went home again, except briefly. Met a Dixie peach in the South Pacific, and within three months you were married and starting a family of your own. Fast operator.

Four kids in no time, and the pressure cranking up and up. Mother drank aftershave and Listerine when she couldn't get anything better, or we kids had hidden or poured away the liquor, but you stuck to gin, and not till six o'clock. The military life. Sometimes you would imagine you were a boy again, could shine again, the world awaiting. But by then you'd been nearly everywhere, and had found nothing that seemed of any real use. The thing you came to value most in the world was the driest of dry Martinis, just a lidful of vermouth, and enough of them to make you sleep all night through.

But there were nights when nothing worked, when the gin didn't kick in quick enough and the stirring, stirring drove you crazy. Then you'd somehow mask your face, dull your features, and climb the stairs quietly, stopping at my bedroom door. You'd open it quietly, letting the light from the stairs into the dark, then shut it again behind you and feel your way over to my bed. I'd be clutched, curled tight as a tiny fist in the dark tent of the covers, dreading my dreams.

I can still see that face, and it's still not quite yours.

You're old and tired now, and it was such a long time ago. *Hell's bells*, you'll be thinking, *can't she just leave me alone?* Hold on, Daddy. I don't want to trouble you, or anyone else for that matter. I just want to connect, but from a distance. My connection with you is too full of crackle and hiss; I want to clear the line, but I'm not sure I can do that without your help. I'm just so sad most of the time that it scares me, this swallow-you-whole sadness is too much for me to bear, and I just keep getting sadder. My marriage hasn't survived it, and I'm not sure I'm going to.

You'll need to move to the big chair now, and turn the heating pad on for your back. You'll be feeling anxious and disturbed, but you won't be unaware of the inevitability of all this, so there will be a kind of relief too. As you settle back, a slight groan will escape your lips, and you'll shut your eyes for a minute, hoping for Istanbul or Tokyo, but all you'll see is me. Oh boy oh boy, Daddy. You've really been around, haven't you?

Home Time

I got home from school and dumped my stuff on the dining-room table. High school was a nightmare for me. I did well enough, but the social effort was punishing. I smiled at everybody till I thought my face would crack. I had to hide the snakes in my belly under as much sweetness as possible. I played an innocent, although I knew I wasn't innocent at all. GUILTY. Of what, I didn't know. But I knew I was guilty as sin, and I must hide it. Home wasn't much better, but at least at home I didn't have to smile all the time.

The smell was there, biting into my eyes and scalp. Mama sat curled like a sleepy but dangerous cat in her chair, which was pockmarked with burn scars, like her bathrobe. *Well well well*, she slurred, *look what's here.* Tildy's tongue was green – Clorets, 'Tastes like a mint, works like a miracle.' Not quite, I thought.

The room was a mess of ash and butts and books and magazines. Gin, Camels, and bitter rage – a bouquet so powerful it seemed to streak the air.

I knew Daddy was coming home tonight. He'd been in Los Angeles for two weeks. Looked like Bubba would have to pick him up. I would get my licence this summer, on my sixteenth birthday. I took my stuff to my room and changed clothes. Better clean up some or Daddy'd have an even bigger fit.

I got the duster from under the sink in the kitchen. It was even worse in the kitchen; my feet made a ripping noise as I lifted them off of the sticky floor and headed for the family room. What was it? Not gin. Maybe orange juice or Coke, I couldn't tell.

I started emptying ashtrays and straightening up. Tildy's firecracker eyes followed me around the room. *Be nice if you helped out all the time, Sugar. No wonder I drink.* I felt stung with shame. My mother was right. I only cleaned when there was a risk of somebody's wrath. Most of the time I kept out of the way, in my room.

My room was upstairs at the front of the house. It faced out into a leafy street of nearly identical houses, all nearly new, and many occupied by military families. There was a double bed, a desk, a chest of drawers, and a dressing table with a three-part mirror. I spent hours just sitting in front of the mirror, trying to see myself, but I couldn't. My bedstead had a built-in shelf upon which sat a pink plastic radio alarm clock and several books. I was reading Hermann Hesse at the time. *Steppenwolf.*

Tildy stood up unsteadily. *Coffee, I need some coffee.* She wobbled towards the kitchen. Her bathrobe fell open to reveal a slip stained with urine. I hated that part, the clean-up part. It was only possible when Tildy was passed out, and it wasn't a pleasant task. I couldn't believe I'd come out of that place.

I watched my mother go to the kitchen and heard her fill the kettle. *Maybe she'll sober up, please, God.* That was another sin; I only ever prayed to God when I wanted something. I went on cleaning up the mess.

Joe

Joe didn't keep a journal, but he kept a scrapbook of murders. He was fascinated by killers, and had been in correspondence with a death row inmate in Texas for over ten years. Bucky Bucknell was his name, and he was in for murdering his mother with a nine-pound hammer. She had been unrecognizable after the event, face smashed to pieces.

Bucky had managed to avoid the lethal injection for so long because he had a friend in local politics who kept holding up the appeal process. His story was that his mother drove him to it; everybody knew she was a nagging, humiliating, royal pain in the butt. He'd pleaded temporary insanity, and was trying to plead it again. His letters to Joe, however, were lucid and full of the gory details of prison life. Bucky was a staunch supporter of the Aryan Ass-Kickers (AAK); had to be in this hell-hole, grossly over-populated with blacks who could really get to you if you didn't stick together.

'Letter from Bucky?' I asked. Joe had just slouched into the living room with the mail in his hand. He was six foot one and had to duck under the doorframe in this old concrete box of a flat. I recognized the pale blue airletter paper.

'Uh-huh.' Joe put the letter in his pocket for later. It was a personal relationship, his and Bucky's: he didn't like sharing it. He picked up five-month-old Claire from the rug she was lying on and threw her gently into the air. She loved that. 'Go for a walk?'

'Yeah. The park?'

'Let's go.'

It was late March and there were daffodils everywhere. The sun was shining and I thought, *I've never been so happy, how has this happened? This perfection?*

We walked around the park and sat on a bench, watching other parents with toddlers on the swings and slides and climbing frames.

'Susie?'

'Yeah?'

Joe fiddled with the bobble on his jacket zipper. 'I've got to tell you something.'

'Go on.' I had gotten my leaking breast out at Claire's prodding and was feeding her.

'I've known . . . I've always known . . . that I won't live past thirty-six.' He put his arm around my shoulders. 'I want to tell you this now, so you'll know it's not your fault. It's just something . . . I've got to do . . . I've always known.'

I was stunned. 'What?' Had I heard him right?

Joe said nothing.

'You're telling me you intend to abandon your daughter when she's eight years old? And what about me?' I felt hysteria creeping up my back, up my neck. My scalp was tingling. Claire started to cry; I was hugging her too tight. 'OK, it's OK,' I loosened my grip and Claire quietened immediately, her attention on her sucking.

Joe got up and said, 'Don't feel bad about it. Maybe I shouldn't have said . . .'

I thought, this is just another one of his weird ideas. Claire will keep him grounded. She'll keep him with us. He'll get over it. I buttoned up my blouse and lifted Claire towards Joe. 'Do you want to take her?'

'Not now. I'll see you back at home. I need to pick something up from my office.' He walked out of the park with a spring in his step. He wanted to read Bucky's letter alone.

The Bridge

It was snowing in Washington DC. It had been snowing for a week already, and schools were closed. It was the heaviest snowfall the region had seen in decades, and the city was ill-equipped to cope. Kids were loving it, even us. There was something clear and fungicidal about snow, especially this take-no-prisoners onslaught of the stuff.

Daddy's flight back from London had been delayed and delayed again, but was finally scheduled for arrival that night at nine. Tildy wouldn't be making the drive, so Bubba and I went together. Sometimes he preferred to go alone and whistle at the girls who passed in their convertibles, but this was hardly the weather for it, and the roads weren't going to be easy to navigate. So he asked me to come with him. The twins would stay home and try to make sure Tildy didn't burn the house down, although, if Tildy had wanted to set us all alight, I'm sure she could have achieved it. They stayed home, anyway, counting their gopher tails and keeping an eye out.

The new airport was right smack dab in the middle of nowhere. The long dark road that led there could be scary. Once, I remember, we were speeding along and one of us suggested that there might be someone hiding in the back of the car. Right behind us. Waiting for the moment to leap up screaming. We got so scared we couldn't even turn our heads. Finally, Bubba slammed on the brakes and put the car in park. I was fixing to faint. He got out and opened the back door. I could see his fingers trembling when I eased my head around towards the back seat, expecting the worst. Of course, there was no one there. We felt so dumb.

On this particular snowy night we took a back route to the airport road. The trees were beautiful, swaying and sparkling like silver in the headlights. A racoon sidled alongside of us briefly. It was icy and Bubba was taking it easy, easy enough, until we got to our favourite place. This was an old stone hump-backed bridge, one lane wide. It was on top of a little hill, so you had to climb up to it and ease down the other side. There was no traffic light or waiting system. You had to stop and make sure no one was coming the other way before crossing.

'Shall we do it?' Bubba whispered. He glanced my way.

I looked straight ahead, nodding.

Bubba stepped on the gas. We slid up the incline and over the bridge, gathering speed on the downhill so that for a second or two, we were flying. The car hit the road again, going into a spin which Bubba corrected like an ace. We drifted to a halt.

'I love that,' I said. 'I just love that.'

'Yeah, well,' Bubba drove on, 'we should probably cut it out.'

I hugged my bony frame, shivering. It was so cold there was ice on the inside of the windshield.

When we got to the airport Daddy was just coming through the gate. His eyes were bleary and he reeked of gin and smoke, but he was grinning wildly. He shoved his brief-case into Bubba's arms and gathered me into a clumsy hug. I felt his breath on my neck and it tickled. I tried to pull my head away and then froze as I felt his tongue slobbering its way up my jawbone. I couldn't think any more. Something was shutting down.

Bubba yanked my arm so hard it hurt. Daddy lost his grip and looked for a second like falling down.

'Well, I'll be damned.' He stood there, looking from me to Bubba and back again. 'Let's go.'

He took his case from Bubba and strode ahead into the parking lot, though he didn't know where the car was. We'd have to show him the way. The good news was he'd probably sleep the whole way home, and I'd be the terrifying stranger hidden in the back seat, waiting for my moment to strike.

Dream

I am lying on my back in a crib, maybe eighteen months old. My daddy is coming towards me from the doorway. He is wearing pyjama bottoms but no top, and on his head is a diaper, folded. He's wearing it like a hat. I can smell it. The diaper pin is blue.

He stands over me, looking down at my stomach. He is gripping the crib with both hands. He starts crooning, Hush-a-bye my baby, slumber time is coming soon. *Just that line, over and over. As he sings, he starts to cry. The teardrops splash on to my belly in a torrent. He takes the diaper off of his head and wipes me dry. Don't cry, he says. But I'm not the one who's crying.*

Bubba Goes to College

By the time Bubba went away to college, none of us had been in much detailed communication with each other for years, probably since the onset of puberty. We had all retreated silently screaming into our own corners, licking our wounds and trying to cope with our hormones. Tildy just got worse; she could hardly bear to look at her children, let alone feed them or speak to them. She was in a long skid that would end only in her death, for which none of her children would be present.

I was in my senior year of high school. The twins were freshmen, and Fred was already getting noticed as a top athlete. But the school we went to was so huge, we rarely even glimpsed each other in the hallways. Daddy came home from work, drank until he fell asleep in his chair, and then took himself to bed sometime in the middle of the night. Very occasionally we all ate dinner together; these were forced and fruitless attempts to be normal. Daddy demanded smiles all around, which we were incapable of providing with any consistency, so an air of disappointment hung over the table like a hot mist. We couldn't see each other through it.

There was some solace in the TV. *Bonanza* was big then, and *Rowan and Martin's Laugh In*. I wished I was pretty and ditzy and knock-kneed like Goldie Hawn. All she had to do was stand there and giggle and everybody loved her. I couldn't even laugh; I never learned to laugh out loud until I was forty years old. Bubba had the same problem, but we only discussed it much much later.

One late afternoon when Tildy and Daddy were both out, Bubba phoned from his college dormitory. Our father had asked him to call once a month so Daddy would know if Bubba had gotten the cheque Daddy sent him. Frank answered, and was talking to Bubba on the kitchen phone when I walked in. Brother was laughing, and looking right at me. 'She sure is, you got that right!' he said.

'Who is it?'

'Bubba.'

'What's so funny?' I felt a desperate unease.

'Nothin'.'

T'other was reading *Sports Illustrated* at the table.

'Freddie, what're they laughing about, huh? Tell me.'

T'other didn't look up from his magazine, just said quietly, 'They're laughing at you, 'cause you're crazy. Don't sweat it.'

I turned and ran. I ran out of the front door and all the way to the creek on the edge of our housing estate. I sat down on the bank and picked a dogwood twig up off of the ground. It was cold, and I hadn't put my coat on. The narrow rivulet beside me had frozen in a kaleidoscopic pattern, with what looked like geometric white clouds suspended in clear ice. It was beautiful. I started scratching at it with my twig. The scratchings turned into *C-R-A-Z-Y C-R-A-Z-Y C-R-A-Z-Y* until the surface was covered. I made one small nick in the palm of my hand, where it wouldn't show. It didn't bleed much; my hands were numb. I'd save the rest for later.

When I got home it was dark. The twins were watching *The Dick Van Dyke Show*. Tildy and Daddy were still out. I went to my room and sat in front of my dressing-table mirror, peering at my missing face, wondering if I'd ever be able to have a husband and a child and a sense of humour.

Susie and Claire

I washed my tired hair under the tired taps, wondering why in such a drenched and mossy country was there no water pressure to speak of, only the drip drip of a leaky tap? It didn't make sense. And then, trying to dry my frizzy Bozo mop – that was another nightmare. Everything seemed always slightly damp in this windy old house, with its primitive gas fires and two holes in its roof. We were renting it for next to nothing, though. And rightly so; it was falling apart.

We were trying half-heartedly to find a house to buy. Did we really want to become home-owners now? Wouldn't the urge to move on come soon? I had always lived a migrant life, first due to Daddy's work, and then just out of habit. I didn't want to get stuck with a mortgage. But, with a kid, accommodation wasn't that easy to come by. It was looking like we'd have to buy, if we could find a house we could afford.

I wrapped a faded towel round my head and scooted into

the bedroom. It was nearly time to get Claire from the nursery, so I'd have to hurry. I put on jeans and a T-shirt, rubbed my head as hard as I could to dry my hair and then left it to do what it wanted. I put on the yellow clogs, grabbed my bag, and left.

When I got to the school, Claire was riding a tricycle furiously around in circles in the yard with her friend Joey. I approached Mrs Tryer, the teacher, and said, *No major disasters, I hope?*

A few spats over the new scooter, but no broken bones, she answered, *and Claire's fine.*

I had never stopped wondering how things had managed to turn out OK. The miraculous had been achieved. Claire was fine, and I loved her easily, breathlessly, shudderingly. How had my own mother avoided it so completely, such an overwhelming and consuming instinct? I had been sure that I had inherited some genetic child rejection syndrome. I'd been terrified at the idea of having kids for this reason; I didn't know what I might do to them. But on Claire's arrival I had felt a euphoria like nothing I could have imagined. I would sit, feeding her first from one enormous breast and then the other, and shudders of love would overcome me to the extent that I was afraid to move. It was almost weird.

When I phoned my mother, asking *When was I weaned? What did I eat first? Say first?* and so on, Tildy just said, *Sugar, as for the birth, I told 'em to put me out cold and then let me know when it was over. As for the rest, I don't remember. Only you weren't breastfed. I tried it with Bubba but he bit me.*

Claire came running up to me and thrust her coat into my hands. *She won't keep it on,* Mrs Tryer said. *I've had to bend the rules a little with Claire.* I took my daughter by the hand. Claire was wearing a flowery skirt over striped trousers, and odd socks, one orange and one blue. In her hair were thirteen hair clips, with all manner of flora and fauna represented on them. The giraffes were her favourites at the moment, so they were prominent, holding back her bangs. *And her head looks just like a dressing table*, Mrs Tryer added. Claire giggled, and headed for the car. *Don't worry, she's hot-blooded*, I smiled, and rattled my keys at Claire. *You'll have to wait for me!* I called. We got in the car and headed home.

I was tired because I was working nights in a pizza place. It was hard work and a late finish, but I wanted to be with Claire in the day, and besides, there wasn't much else I could do in this foreign city. I had a degree, but no other qualification, and the economy was pretty depressed. Joe's job didn't pay much, and we needed two incomes if we were going to buy a house.

As we headed for home, I wondered what to make for dinner. It was my turn to cook. I knew we had some pasta, there were eggs, and some cheese . . . *Sausages*, Claire said. My hair stood even further on end. *How do you do that, Claire? You do that all the time!*

I dunno. Claire was rearranging her hair clips. She started singing 'Bobby Shafto'. I guessed that the young were generally more sensitive, or more in touch with their primitive natures. But telepathic? Were they all like that? Had I been once? Could adults regain that skill if they tried?

OK, sausages then. With what else?

Mashed potatoes and ice cream. Claire giggled her hiccupy Claire giggle. I felt a love-shudder, which I had continued to do occasionally since those first months. But I never could understand the undercurrent of fear that accompanied them, every time.

I love you too, you and Bobby Shafto. Claire sang all the way home.

I was cooking sausages when Joe came in. He didn't say anything, just got the *Guardian* and started the quick crossword at the kitchen table. Claire was in the garden perfecting her skipping technique, which involved holding both hands up in the air, as if she were about to conduct a symphony. Summer was coming, and it was still light outside. The clematis was showing new buds, and birds were singing. It was a beautiful evening.

I can't eat that crap. Joe slapped the paper down. *You know I'm in training.* Joe was a runner, and did as many marathons as he could each year. The next one was in two weeks. Truth was, Joe was obsessed with his diet, but his dietary obsessions could change overnight. One week he might be a vegetarian, the next he would insist that meat is the only proper protein for an athlete. Life was always easier when he cooked.

It was Claire's request. Had a bad day? I turned the sausages and checked the potatoes. Our second-hand stove was unpredictable. It seemed to be able to turn itself off and on. Twice I'd come downstairs in the morning to find the back burner lit.

Joe growled. *Not until now.* He got up and left the room.

I knew what the trouble was. I also knew that a solution was not looking likely anytime soon. I'd gone off sex, and that he considered part of his training too.

I remember the first time I had sex. I was closed so tight it took the poor guy hours to get inside. When he finally did and there was no hymenal blood, he eyed me with furious suspicion, put on his flares and went. I think he was collecting virgins. I was ashamed. I had failed all round.

When I met Joe, we were friends for months before we made love, and when we finally did, I conceived almost immediately. This, although a shock at the time (diaphragm failure), somehow legitimized sexual intercourse for me. I was righteous in my desire, because I was a mother.

It was now, when Claire was a walking talking bucketful of her own beans, that the feeling of legitimacy had abandoned me. It wasn't OK any more, and I couldn't go back to my blank-it-all-out approach. Too much had occurred in my nether regions; I had woken up down there, and I wanted to stay awake. But I didn't want to do it with the father of my child. It didn't seem right. I couldn't explain it to Joe or even myself and make sense. So we were stuck, and neither one of us knew what to do.

I mashed the potatoes and called Claire in. She asked where her daddy was and I told her he was on his way, but we should eat while it was hot. We both heard the front door slam. *Daddy's gone running. The marathon's in two weeks.*

Can I have his sausages? For Bubble and Squeak?

Gerbils don't eat sausages, Claire. They're vegetarians.

I could just see if they will, couldn't I?

All right, sweetie, but you won't have much luck.

We ate, and then Claire tried to get her gerbils to eat sausages while I scraped at fat and gristle under a lukewarm drippy tap.

The Dummy

The kids were all at school and Walt had left for Tokyo the night before. He'd be gone three weeks this time, *not nearly long enough*, Tildy thought, as she stuffed sheets into the washer. She was down in the basement, her favourite place in this tract house that was too square and hot for Tildy's taste. She preferred cool and curving, like the back of a snake.

Tildy switched the machine on and sat down at her dressmaker's table – a long piece of plywood held up by three sawhorses and covered in patterns and pins and tape measures and books and ashtrays. Her Bible was open at Isaiah: COME DOWN AND SIT IN THE DUST O VIRGIN DAUGHTER OF BABYLON . . . THY NAKEDNESS SHALL BE UNCOVERED, YEA, THY SHAME SHALL BE SEEN . . . *Oh, no, I'm not getting into THAT*, she thought, and quickly flipped the pages and settled on Philippians: WHATSOEVER THINGS ARE TRUE . . . HONEST . . . JUST . . .

PURE ... LOVELY ... OF GOOD REPORT; IF THERE BE ANY VIRTUE, AND IF THERE BE ANY PRAISE, THINK ON THESE THINGS. She was determined to pray and stay positive until The Word regained some of its former power for her. Her passionate love of God had been a rock to stand on, like they say. Now she was stuck and sinking in the purgatorial quicksand of the faithless. She couldn't get the glory back.

Tildy had been attending AA meetings for about six months. She hadn't touched a drop, never mind Walt paralysing himself with dry Martinis every night as usual. Now he was gone, she was determined to study and sew, study and sew, and stay sober. She'd made it through a morning and most of an afternoon.

She pushed the book aside and picked up her newest Vogue pattern. It was for a tailored suit, a pencil-thin skirt with a neat slit up the back, and a jacket nipped in at the waist, double breasted with wide lapels. She'd bought some beautiful navy blue linen and six shiny gold buttons, and her brand-new dressmaker's dummy was standing in wait, adjusted to Tildy's petite proportions. She had never attempted real tailoring before. This would be yet another string to her bow.

When the table was cleared and the fabric spread out, she started pinning the pattern pieces on to the cloth. She thought of the AA meetings, full of losers and whiners, not like herself at all. She hated them.

Susie went with her to these meetings. Tildy had asked her. She wanted Susie to drive. Tildy's night vision was getting bad. So they went together, every Tuesday night, to the Methodist church community hall, to listen to stories: *It started with a couple a drinks after work with the boys. Pretty soon*

I wasn't going home at all . . . My husband left me with three kids and a bad case of clap. I had no idea he was . . . It creeps up, and before you know it, you're stealing money from the kids' piggy banks . . . I had bottles hidden all over the house . . . I swear, I never saw the kid. I tried to swerve, but it happened so fast . . . and so on. Tildy never told her story. She grimaced through these sad accounts, but always cried when she had to introduce herself as an alcoholic, bitter and furious tears, because she never really believed she was one, even though you had to say so to attend the meetings.

And that pathetic Susie, sitting there smug as shit, Tildy thought, *I don't know why I let her come. Little slut.* Tildy pricked her finger with a pin. She put it into her mouth quickly, but not quickly enough to prevent drops of blood spotting the linen. *DAMN IT TO HELL!! GODDAMNIT!!* Tildy swore, holding her finger in the air. She felt tears pricking at her eyelids. *Nothing goes right, nothing, nothing, nothing.*

She pushed the fabric aside and lit a cigarette. *Get a Goddamn grip,* she told herself. The washer was nearing the end of its cycle. She would put the clothes in the dryer and then go upstairs and sweep the floors. It was Tuesday, meeting night, so she'd better start thinking about a quick and easy dinner.

But the tears wouldn't go away. Tildy's heartache always translated itself into homesick blues at times like this, so she thought of Texas and her fervent wish that she had never left it, never met Walt, never borne his useless and ungrateful children. Never gotten old and worn like her daddy's Chevy, just spluttering along out of tune and out of style. How could all this have happened to the snazziest girl in Windville? *HOW?*

Almost without thinking Tildy began rummaging in the ragbag she kept under the table, full of dressmaking scraps and old sheets and towels. She found the bottle and pulled it out, a fifth of Beefeaters. She calculated, trying to recall exactly what her resources were, and where. She could remember one in the bottom of her dirty clothes hamper, and one in a hatbox in her bedroom closet, as well as the gallon Walt kept in the liquor cabinet. She'd be OK for a while.

Tildy emptied the dregs from her coffee cup into the utility sink and poured herself a generous shot. She relished the herby gin smell; she could feel the hit of it even before she downed the drink in one. She poured another, bigger shot and sipped it slowly. As she drank, she pulled the pin cushion close and started sticking pins one by one into the dummy's breasts. *One for you and one for you and another and another and another* . . . until the pins were all used up. She poured another drink and lit another cigarette, gazing with admiration at the newly chain-mailed, breast-plated model of herself. She felt better.

Susie found her mama slumped at her table, passed out and dribbling on to the navy blue linen, the empty bottle beside her. *No meeting tonight*, she thought. *And probably not for a while*.

They never did go again. But Tildy finished her suit eventually, and it was stunning. At least one neighbour borrowed the pattern. Mrs Schmidt's was made up in pale pink. But it would never look as good on her as it did on Tildy.

Houston

I didn't tend to spend much time alone with my mother. There were too many of us, and there was rarely a reason to make the effort, except for medical visits. Tildy used to take me to the orthodontist by the back routes. We'd kind of feel our way around the country lanes, avoiding the traffic of the big city. Tildy said to me once, 'I like driving you. You don't mind getting lost.' A compliment. I was so taken aback that I didn't speak for the remainder of the journey. I felt proud of myself; I had a good trait, not minding getting lost. My mama liked something about me.

So, it felt extremely odd to be travelling to Houston alone with Tildy. I was eighteen, just out of high school and ready to start college in the fall. Her father was ill, dying, and it was agreed that I would go with her to see out Grandpa's last weeks. This was women's work. The others would drive down for the funeral, and we'd all drive home together.

Tildy was in tears for most of the flight, so there was not much room for conversation. I didn't know how to comfort her; it was odd to see her so brimming with love and grief. These were not emotions I associated with my mother. She also refused an in-flight cocktail, which I thought was a worrying sign. We were in for a sober time. It was during her periods of sobriety that Tildy was at her fiercest. She was a martyr, and she bled at top volume. When I was younger, of course I preferred her sober at any cost. Now it wasn't so clear.

Aunt Gracie picked us up at the airport. Tildy was the oldest of four girls. Gracie came next, then Wynne, and finally Patricia, or Popsy as she was called. Gracie was slim and elegant and beside herself. The sisters hugged each other tight, sniffling into each other's necks. They were the same five foot two, with the same high cheekbones and almost black eyes, only Gracie looked rosy while Tildy was beginning to crease and crack around the edges. By the time Tildy died, she looked old enough to be Gracie's mother, even though there was only a year between them.

The heat shimmered up off the I-45 as we headed south towards Telephone Road. Tildy sat in the front with Gracie, who filled her in on Grandpa's condition. He was suffering from a wasting of the nerves, and had pretty much lost all nervous control. He couldn't speak, and was hooked up to all kinds of machines that had taken over his bodily functions. It wouldn't be long. Gracie let out a sob. 'We're taking it in shifts at the hospital, two at a time. Then come back to the house, eat, sleep, you know. People have been great, the food just keeps coming. Haven't had to worry . . .' Tildy had stopped crying now. She gripped her Kleenex. The indignity of this death, her daddy, her proud and stubborn, her funny and tender Indian daddy, it wasn't right. *Life stinks*, she thought, *it Goddamn stinks.*

When we pulled up in front of the house, Wynne's youngest, Johnny, was swinging on the porch swing. He jumped up, waving wildly, and ran in to tell the others we were here. Grandma appeared first, wringing a tea towel in her hands. She looked exhausted. Wynne followed her out and came down the steps to greet us. Johnny was at her heels. He was five years old and like a Mexican jumping bean; he never stopped moving.

'Y'all got here OK? Come on in and have some iced tea. There's lots to eat.' Wynne put her arm around Tildy's shoulder and gave her a squeeze. 'Susie, how you doin', Sugar?' She winked at me, smiling, but the signs of strain were obvious. Wynne had the roundest, softest face of the four sisters, and the fairest complexion. She was maternal by nature, like Grandma, with none of the snap and crackle of the others. She had four children; Johnny was the youngest, and not in school yet. The rest she'd left at home in Beaumont with their daddy, my Uncle Raul.

We went up on the porch, and Tildy hugged her mother. Grandma seemed so frail. Her normally sturdy body was shrunken and stooped with worry. She said, 'Tildy honey, thank God. Daddy's been asking for you.' This brought tears to Tildy's eyes again. She would spend these few weeks reeling between rage and grief, and taking me with her.

We entered the house, walked through the cluttered front room to the kitchen at the back. The table was extended to its full length, and piled high with food. There were sweet-potato pie, pecan pie, two big hams, bowls of fried chicken and potato salad, creamed corn, hush puppies, breaded okra, black-eyed peas with salt pork, corn bread, slices of watermelon, and more.

'The neighbours have been busy. Everybody's been so sweet.' Wynne handed Tildy and me a plate each, but Tildy refused hers.

'I want to go to the hospital now,' she said.

'Popsy's there. She'd be glad to see you. Don't you want to get ready first?' Gracie asked.

'I am ready. Mother, do you want to come with me?'

'She's just come back. She needs to sleep,' Wynne answered. 'I'll come. I've had a rest.'

'I'll come if you want me to, Tildy.' Grandma started to untie her apron strings.

'No, Mother, you stay here. I'll go ahead with Wynne.'

They left in Grandpa's rattling smoking old '57 Chevy. The sisters had been trying to talk him into trading it in for years, but Grandpa refused. He called it Henrietta; he said, 'She knows my moods.'

I didn't see my grandfather until three days later, and by then he couldn't communicate at all. He recognized me, I think. I had been on kitchen and Johnny duty. I greeted visitors and accepted their gifts of food, offering them plates and glasses of tea, chatted with them while they ate, and washed the dishes when they left. There was a steady flow of company. They all whispered, 'You must be Tildy's girl, you look just like her.' We had to keep quiet, because there was always somebody sleeping, in between trips to the hospital.

Keeping Johnny quiet was another story. He was a rascal, fond of lighting matches and squealing like a scalped cavalryman. He was three feet tall and a million feet BIG. He got on my nerves. I'd never been responsible for a child before, except for the twins, and he knew it too. I threatened, and bribed, and pleaded, and scolded, but he kept his antics up. I couldn't tell Aunt Wynne; she had enough to think about.

After about a week of this routine, I snapped. Popsy and Grandma were asleep in the front bedroom, I was washing the millionth dish that day, and Johnny was squealing away under the table. 'Stop that this red hot minute!' I hissed, and the plate in my hands cracked clean in two. I didn't even dry off, just grabbed Johnny by the arm, and the first thing I saw to hit him with, a wooden yardstick. I yanked him out of the house and started down the street with him.

'I'm not gonna whip you here and wake Popsy and Grandma. I'm gonna whip you away from the house, I'm gonna really whip you hard.' I dragged him along, and aimed my first blow at his legs. The yardstick broke in two, so I carried on with my hands. I must've hit him ten or twelve times, only on his legs. I wasn't strong or experienced enough to do any damage, but by the time I'd finished he was quiet.

'Do you understand me?' I asked him.

'Uh-huh,' he answered.

He followed me back to the house. In fact, he followed me everywhere from then on, and didn't act up again. Our friendship was firmly cemented, born of an act of frustrated violence. We laugh about it now.

My mother and I went for walks some days or evenings. She would point out the places where she played as a child, the old movie theatre, dilapidated now and up for sale, the best climbing tree in the neighbourhood. We walked by her high school and looked in the windows. Tildy had gone to grade school in Windville, before the family had moved to Houston.

Houston was so much smaller then, people knew each other, she told me, with a desperate heartache in her voice. *She knows she's blown it*, I thought, amazed, *she knows it*. Tildy was in the habit of blaming everyone else for her troubles.

One evening we went downtown to Buffalo Bayou, near Montrose. We walked along the water in the lingering heat of the sunset. Folks were whizzing by on bicycles, or jogging in pairs. There were long-haired men and braless women walking arm-in-arm. There were gay couples holding hands, though not as many as you'd see today. My mother couldn't get used to all this freedom of expression. Her frown deepened as we walked. A couple passed us, a man and woman in their early twenties, she with her hand in his hip pocket, and he with his hand curled round her back and under her arm, stroking her erect nipple. They giggled on by, and Tildy asked me abruptly if I had 'done it' yet, and how often and with whom. I was so surprised I tripped, nearly fell into the bayou. We had never talked about much of anything, never mind real intimacies. I said no, and she said, 'Yes, sure.' She didn't believe me. This was the swinging sixties, after all. What Tildy didn't know was that I had a reputation for being the most frigid girl in my class. I couldn't stand the idea of some boy's hands or lips touching me, and everybody knew it, as everybody always does. I couldn't tell her that. I preferred her to think me promiscuous. 'I've only ever known your father,' she spat. She was jealous! Jealous of what she thought were my life and times. I was getting to know my mother a little bit better.

Grandpa died on the day before my daddy and brothers arrived. It had been a losing battle, but he had fought it anyway, managing to stay alive for three weeks after Mama and I got there. He was in a coma for the last few days, and rapidly declining, so Tildy had told Daddy and the boys to come on ahead, it was time. The drive took three days.

Everybody was pretty cried out by then, and the funeral was a quiet affair. The church was full. In the middle of the eulogy, Tildy whispered to me, 'Susie, see that man over there, with the bald head?' I looked where her head was indicating, across the aisle and back a row, and nodded. 'He asked me to marry him once upon a time, and now he's Mayor.' I didn't know what to say.

We went back to even more food, Frito pie, a huge pot of chilli, frijoles con queso, shrimp gumbo, crawfish and catfish, bisquits and white gravy, pork and beans. People ate, and talked, and went, leaving the family behind in a kind of dumbfounded state. Aunt Wynne packed her husband and kids up and left for Beaumont. Gracie and Popsy both lived in Houston with their families, so they stayed awhile longer. My cousin Etty, Gracie's oldest of two, turned on the TV. We were shocked to hear that Robert Kennedy had been shot that day. These were deadly times.

Tildy and Walt

Try and drink this Ensure, Tildy. Just try. Walt pushed his glasses up his nose and straightened up, feeling an ache in his shoulder. He hadn't been golfing for months. Couldn't raise his arm higher than shoulder level. Anyway, it was getting riskier leaving Tildy on her own. She could barely make it to the toilet without assistance now. She had just turned sixty-six.

I hate Ensure, Goddamnit, Daddy. You know I do. Tildy pouted rather than spat. Walt didn't know which was more aggravating.

If you won't eat your lunch then you have to have something. Walt sighed and put the glass on the table beside his wife. He lit a cigarette. Today was hairdo day. It was the only place she went any more. Her sisters dropped in from time to time, dutifully, but Tildy could barely disguise her impatience with these visits. They wanted something from her that she was incapable of giving. Couldn't they see that? Why couldn't they just leave her alone? And she particularly resented the saint-hood they had bestowed on Walt. *He's a saint*, they all murmured, shaking their heads. He goddamn wasn't. It really got her goat.

It was ten years after the twins left home that Tildy had her first stroke. It was a mild one, but it knocked her out of whack for good. Walt became her nursemaid, and this shift in roles was resonant for both of them. Tildy had the feeling that some kind of atonement was taking place. Walt was grateful for something to do. After retirement he hadn't been able to settle on anything, just prowled the house waiting for the sun to go over the yardarm. Tildy'd hated having him under her feet, and she'd told him so on a daily basis. It was hell. But Tildy's illness had changed all that.

Walt made his way to the kitchen and sat down. He could-n't force-feed her. He shook his head and picked up one of the dozen or so pencils lying on the plastic placemat in the centre of the table. He'd do a bit of his crossword puzzle and try again later.

I love you, Walt, Tildy whimpered from her chair.

I love you too, Mother, Walt muttered automatically, then sighed his hound-dog sigh. *I love you too.*

Half an hour later Walt looked at his watch. *Time to get ready for your hair appointment, Tildy,* he said as he stood up and stretched. He walked to Tildy's chair. She was asleep, snoring faintly through parted lips. Her thick grey hair stood up at odd angles, creating a cubist frame for her wizened face. Her blotchy hands lay folded in her lap. She had always been slim, but now she was brittle and vanishing before his eyes. She had no appetite except for double-chocolate ice cream, which the doctor said was too high in fat and sugar. Walt let her eat some now and then anyway. She couldn't live on air.

He shook her gently by the shoulder. *Come on, Mother. Let's get ready.* Tildy opened her eyes and looked at her husband as if he were a stranger. There was always something that startled her about Walt when she first woke up. But then her mind would go blank, and she'd come around.

With Walt's help Tildy stood and they walked to her bedroom down the hallway. She sat at her vanity table and removed her robe and nightgown while Walt got her clothes ready. She got a bra and some panties out of the bottom drawer. It was convenient to keep them there now.

How's this? Walt asked, holding up a powder blue stretch pantsuit with daisies around the neckline and cuffs.

All right, Tildy answered. She didn't much care any more what she wore. Walt was the one who had to look at her, so he might as well choose to please himself.

She pulled on her undies and put on her bra, which Walt hooked up for her. He handed his wife her pants first and she pulled them up. His fingers stroked her shoulders and his eyes glazed over for a moment. What was the name of that rocky beach in Okinawa? Where he'd first kissed the hot little girl from Texas? What a night that was.

Come on, Walt. We'll be late. Tildy brushed his hands away. *Hand me my top.* Walt did as he was told. When Tildy was dressed she opened her jewellery box and, after careful consideration, took out her pearl ring and a gold chain necklace with a single gold daisy hanging from it.

They got in the car and headed for the beauty parlour. It was raining hard, the tail end of a hurricane that had just missed them this time. Tildy spoke. *I wonder what Susie's husband's really like?*

Walt stiffened in his seat. *Well, Tildy, she said he's a nice boy. A technician, I think she said. Long hair and a beard. But a nice boy.*

Why doesn't she send a picture? Normal people take pictures of their weddings. Something's fishy, I just know it. He must be deformed or something. Tildy snorted. *I bet he's deformed. Little do-gooder. See how she likes living with a deformed husband. Give me a cigarette.* Walt obliged, lighting it first and handing it over. *And what about the children, for God's sake?*

Walt groaned. *I'm sure she would have told us . . .*

She tells us not a Goddamn thing, Walt, and you know it. A secretive girl, always was. Always something to hide.

Walt turned into the parking lot and stopped the car. He led Tildy by the elbow into the shop and left her in the careful hands of Stellabelle Brown. He crossed the street and went into Baskin & Robbins for a two-scoop chocolate-mint-chip cone, which he ate on a stool at the window counter, licking the drips that ran down the side. He wondered who his daughter had married. A man or a mouse? And what would come of it? Walt shuddered. It was a good thing she was over there and not over here. That was one good thing.

He wiped his fingers and the corners of his mouth and threw the crumpled napkin on the counter. He lit a cigarette and pushed his battered golfing hat back on his head. Another fifteen minutes, he thought, and Tildy would be done. *Oh boy oh boy*, he sighed. The kid serving behind the ice-cream counter looked up and Walt stood, embarrassed. He picked up the sticky napkin and placed it deliberately in the trash can by the door, then smiled his toothy smile and waved goodbye as he left. He'd wait it out in the beauty parlour.

On the way home Tildy spoke again. *We should send them a wedding present. We gave Bubba a wedding present, both weddings. That's probably the main reason she got married, so we'd send her a present.*

It's a long way. Maybe some money?

Oh, no. No money.

What then? Walt couldn't imagine what Susie would want, except money.

A framed photograph of her parents. We can send the one we had taken last Christmas at Foleys. Tildy sat back smugly in her seat. *She may be in England but she won't forget those that raised her. And neither will her deformed husband.*

They turned into the driveway. Walt eased the Chrysler into the garage and Tildy into the house, locking everything behind them as he went.

Wheeze III

Your hands are shaking, Daddy, aren't they? I know
about the fall you took last week; Bubba's been keeping
me informed all these years. Ha! Didn't know that, did
you? Bubba loves me Daddy, he really does. So do the
twins, although I talk to them less often. We're
FAMILY, aren't we?

You've got carers in now, I know that too. How you
must hate the intrusion into your twilight time, not to
mention having to admit that you need help. Never
were one to ask for help, like most men of your
generation. It breaks my heart to think about that.

Bubba says Miss G is OK, though. I can just see you
and her sitting side by side in the big sputnik
armchairs, alternately watching TV and dozing off,
cigarettes burning beside you both, often down to the
ash, unsmoked. *Are these your glasses or my glasses?* you'll

ask, attempting to read the TV Chronologue. Your oxygen tank gurgles through the house, like a curlew trapped indoors. Heat, sweat, pictures of generations staring out into rooms full of dust and clutter and the faintest breathing possible. Miss G keeps notes:

9 am: Mr E drinking coffee and smoking. Bad coughing spell, followed by nausea, but won't take Composine.

9:45 am: Mr E worried about the furniture and how he's gonna get it out of here in time. Says, Where are we going? Where are we billeted? How did this house end up here? Mumbling on, despite my reassurances that he's not leaving this house, ever.

1:30 pm: Meatloaf, collards, mashed potatoes, canned peaches. Ate about half; doesn't like collards. Napping now.

And so on, chronicling your hours. There's something slightly skewed in this; now that you do nothing, it's endlessly discussed and noted. And all those years of various and frenzied activity went unremarked. Until now.

Can you remember, Daddy, driving across the desert at night in our old Mercury station wagon, everybody asleep in the back except you and me? You'd drive and I'd 'keep you awake', you said, but really I just couldn't sleep and so we'd sing and sing, and see raindrops the size of baseballs that fell for thirty seconds out of a clear sky and then vanished, or advertisements for three-legged chickens and five-legged cows, or now and then a pair of eyes watching us from the side of the road. We knew all the Burma Shave billboards by heart.

Casey Jones, mounted to the cabin, Casey Jones, with his orders in his hand, Casey Jones, mounted to the cabin and he took his farewell trip to the promised land. How many times did we cross the Mohave in the cool dark night, just you and me awake in the world? They were perfect moments for us, the best. We were going somewhere, in transit, in between, suspended in the safety of forward motion. Nobody could touch us. *Oh my darlin', oh my darlin'* . . . I really cared about you then. And now, but this is a new kind of caring. Rooted in different needs.

Hushabye my baby, slumber time is coming soon. Rest your head upon my breast while Mammy hums a tune . . .You'll need a nap after all this, so you'll stub out your cigarette and turn the heating pad on low, lean back and close your cloggy eyes. With that damn cataract you can't even read any more, and your eyeballs ache like thunder. You'll drift off to Kyoto or Istanbul or Hamburg and be twenty-four again, handsome and winsome in your uniform and wings. Always happiest en route, which is another way of saying nowhere. Prince of the sky.

The last time I saw you, except for very briefly at Mama's funeral, was fifteen years ago. I thought if I came with my own offspring I'd feel like an adult in your house, which seemed to always keep me five years old. My daughter was five then herself, a chattering whizzing dream, a sparkle in the eye of everyone who knew her. When she came skipping through your

living room and you hollered, *SLOW DOWN!*, she
looked at you with some surprise and asked, *Why?* You
went purple and growled, *Do you let her talk to you like
that?* We were all five then.

Later, we went to Aunt Wynne's, and we found her
looking after Mayanne, her granddaughter, who had
swallowed a bottle of her father's anti-psychotic
medication. She'd been rushed to the hospital to have
her stomach pumped, and was weak and wan and
silent. You took her on your knee and cooed, *Now this
is a little sweetieheart. This is an angel of a girl. This is how
a daughter should behave.* Mute and helpless, I thought.
That's how you like them.

I always wondered what Mother knew and didn't
know. Mother with her Indian eyes and snapping
tongue. Mother with enough bitter fury in her to cause
wildlife to panic when she passed. Did you love each
other? You sure did look good together in those old
war photographs, a whirlwind romance in the balmy
but bloody South Pacific, the dark-eyed Dixie Peach
and the rugged Yankee pilot. How these images tear at
us, begging for a plot, or at least a happy ending.

Miss G might be calling you for dinner and meds
now, Daddy. Blood pressure, Beta Blockers, heart, soul
and spleen pills, all to keep you going for a little bit
longer, to keep you in this dreamworld, this rubber-
soled corridor where the temperature is never quite
right. You'll try to eat; you've always taken good care of
yourself, apart from the gin and tobacco, which were
essentials in your line of work, though perhaps
moderation was acceptable? You didn't know how to

manage that. But eating is not the pleasure it once was. It's a damn struggle, in fact. Food just seems to stick in your craw, it won't go down right, and then the nausea attacks and you hang over the trash can you keep beside you, hoping to avoid the disgrace of an upchuck.

Poor you. You were never sick once when collecting corpses, and prided yourself on this fact. Your daddy would have belted you if you had been. He was stern but fair, you always said, though rumours were whispered among the cousins of a sadistic streak. We – Bubba, the twins and I – never knew what to believe. We hardly saw him before he died when we were still in our teens, but he was just a little bit scary. Everyone kept a respectful distance, and he wasn't a back-slapper or even a hand-shaker on greeting. I'm not entirely certain he ever knew my name; he surely never spoke it.

You might be thinking about him as you ease yourself up from the table, taking a fresh toothpick from the USAF shotglass you keep them in and heading for your chair. You'll check the calendar as you pass – *What the Sam Hill am I supposed to be doing today? Is it Thursday?* – and find nothing written there to jog your memory. The truth is, you're going nowhere. After decades of desiring it, needing it desperately, you can finally rest. But it's hard going, this enforced leisure; something itches, something creeps and wags like a crooked finger down your spine. So I'm going to help.

Frank Gordon's Visits

In the months immediately preceding Tildy's death a peculiar phenomenon occurred. Every time she was left alone for more than twenty minutes in the living room, Daddy would return to find her furious. *That Frank Gordon's been here again, pestering me with his talk talk talk. I can't abide that man, damn it to hell, Daddy, why do you let him come? You know I can't stand him.*

Frank and his family had lived next door for about ten years. They were good neighbours, energetic and thoughtful, both keen followers of current events and active in global humanitarian efforts as well as in their church. Tildy had found all this tedious in the extreme and resisted their social efforts, except for the occasional game of bridge with plenty of gin. But three years before, when Frank retired, the family had moved to Muskogee. The house was now occupied by a young Tejano couple, both NASA computer analysts and hardly ever home.

Now, Mother, Daddy would say patiently, *you know Frank and Ilse left Houston three years ago. He couldn't have been here.*

He was here, Goddamnit, what kind of fool do you think I am? I know when someone's standing right in front of me.

Tildy would become so agitated on these occasions that Daddy would give in to her demand for a cigarette, even though the doctor said just one could kill her, her arteries were so bad. She'd go on fussing until Daddy couldn't stand it any more and retreated to the back room with his murder mystery; then, like as not, when he came back they'd go through the whole thing again.

I like the idea of a psychic connection between Frank and Tildy. If opposites do attract, this would be a perfect example: open, sociable, liberal connects with closed, bitter, jaundiced. Maybe they 'did it' one night under the mimosa tree and fell in hopeless love. But it's more likely that Tildy draws Frank across the plains to her chairside with her hatred.

During these months Frank visited at least twice a week, and often more. One time Daddy walked in and heard Tildy muttering angrily, incoherently. When he asked what was the matter, she said, *He brought his GUITAR, for God's sake, he was SINGING, for God's sake, in PORTUGUESE!*

Now, Mother, Daddy sighed, *why would he want to do that?* Daddy had given up reminding her that Frank's presence was a physical impossibility; she wouldn't hear of it anyway.

Give me a cigarette, Tildy answered. Daddy obliged, sucking his bridgework and wondering how to put an end to all this. It was getting him down.

He decided to invite Frank and Ilse down for dinner. They still had a daughter in the area, and could combine visits. Tildy hated visitors, but maybe Frank in the flesh would bring her to her senses. Anyway, it would be nice to socialize for a change. He was almost as sick of his own company as he was tired of Tildy's. He'd get a ready-cooked chicken with all the trimmings from Krogers.

When Ilse answered the phone Daddy could tell something was wrong. Her voice was flat and measured, as if she were counting words. She told Daddy that Frank had had a seizure three months ago, and had been in a coma ever since. It wasn't looking good.

After Daddy told Tildy, she cried and cried. *That man really got on my nerves*, she wailed and snorted. Her tears and complaints gradually juddered to a wheezy halt, and she asked Daddy for a cigarette. *This one could kill you*, Daddy warned. *I know*, Tildy replied, but took it anyway, and rolled it sadly between her fingers.

Tildy decided to die that night, and made her preparations. So did Frank. They were both gone by morning. Daddy cried then, and tears up fast now at the thought of either one of them.

The Goat and Whistle

It had been a hard night, a few really nasty ones in after the football match. United had won, for God's sake. Couldn't they just get happy instead of pig-ignorantly trying to wreck the place?

I'd been working at The Goat and Whistle for three years. Claire was fourteen and blooming, needing me less, and I was considering what to do with the rest of my life. Joe had been promoted and was relatively happy at the university. We hadn't played music together for a few years. Or anything else for that matter. He was very involved with Rhoda, and stayed at her house usually three nights a week. I was seeing Gareth. Joe and I were getting along OK. We felt very grown up, and a bit Bohemian about our unconventional lifestyle. I couldn't see that I was treating my body like it wasn't connected to me at all, back to eyes-shut unconscious coupling with anyone who asked, just to prove I wasn't frigid.

Gareth was a painter. He was the only child of a loving mother and a coldly neglectful father who had been a miner, and had died of pneumoconiosis when Gareth was twenty-eight. Gareth had inherited his artistic talent from his father, who used to draw beautifully detailed scenes from nature. But he had never approved of Gareth's choice of profession; painting was a hobby, and unless you were Lowry, you should work for a living like a real man. When he died, Gareth was left with a kind of frustrated fury, which he tried to spend on his work, but usually ended up taking out on women, excepting his mother, whom he adored.

I met Gareth in The Goat and Whistle, which was his local. He always stayed for the lock-in after closing with the small group of regulars approved by Jez, the landlord. I started staying too, at his urging, and we became involved. This meant staying late two or three nights a week, drinking lots of strong lager, and having sex in the back of his van. Sometimes the sun was coming up when I got home.

'You're pretty, sweetheart. Have you got a light?' He was clearly a rogue, but he made me laugh. And what was more, we looked alike. People used to ask if he was my brother. It was uncanny. But we did feel related, somehow. He called me his soulmate, and sometimes his wife.

Gareth taught me how to drink, and introduced me to the pleasures of heroin and blueys and poppers, especially when employed prior to, or during, sexual intercourse. He was like an image of myself in negative, or the other side of the coin. He opened a door in my underbelly that had been locked tight, and he did it easily, just like the way he'd slide his hand down the back of my jeans and hold it on my naked hip, wherever we were. An act of ownership; it drove me crazy with lust.

It was a kind of sexual control that made me floppy and confused. I'd never felt anything like it, as far as I could remember.

Then one night he hit me. It was after midnight. I was sitting crosslegged on the leather bench, talking to Jez about extending the pub, when he came up and whacked me on the side of the head. 'Don't sit like that. You're sitting like a fucking whore.'

I started crying. I hadn't been hit since I was a child. Jez and some others got Gareth out of there. Jez dried my eyes and talked to me till two am. He told me Gareth was nuts and everybody knew it, I should get rid of him, look at the way he treats you, you deserve better, and anyway what are you doing with your life? Jez was everybody's idea of a really nice guy. He had a perfect wife and two perfect kids, and gave big bonuses on the birthdays of his staff. I was grateful.

I left the pub and headed for my car. Gareth was waiting for me there. He grabbed me by the shoulders and started licking my neck, breathing hot words, *Fuck me, Susie, fuck me, I want to fuck you, I need to fuck you, you cunt*. We got into the back of the car and went at it with heightened and delirious passion. We were transformed. The difference: I was shudderingly, sickeningly terrified throughout. It was weirdly familiar, like your mother's perfume but on someone else's skin.

We carried on like this for two years. There'd be weeks when I'd refuse to see him ever again. I'd change my shifts at work to avoid him, and not answer the phone at home. But he'd always win me around again with his 'We're soulmates, I need you, there's nothing you can do about it.' I think I wanted to believe in the fateful nature of our love. I wanted it to be 'bigger than both of us', because then I couldn't question remaining in such a damaging relationship; there'd be no point.

Gareth's outbursts of violence were unpredictable, as were his outbursts of affection. He could be almost unbearably tender, holding my hand under the table or putting new strings on my guitar. I used to dream of him as a woman. He wasn't very tall, but he was solidly built, almost barrel chested. It was the way he moved his hands, I think, sort of fluttery. In my dreams he was always wearing a dress, smiling. In one, he was running through a meadow with his arms full of flowers, wearing a red knee-length shift. I was never present in these dreams, except as an observer. Or maybe I was *being* Gareth; I don't know.

On our last night together, we were just leaving The Goat when he hit me so hard I passed out. I don't remember why; there usually wasn't an obvious reason. When I came around, I was lying on the bench. Jez was sitting next to me. We were alone in the pub. He handed me a cup of tea.

'Sit up and drink this. You'll feel better.'

My nose was swollen and I couldn't open one eye. All I could think about was what I'd tell Claire. I drank the tea while Jez made soothing noises. He also said, 'This is it, Susie. You've got to get rid of that pillock. It can't go on any longer. The man's gonna kill you one day.'

I sobbed and sniffed, and Jez stroked my leg. I realized too late that he'd gotten his penis out and was stroking that too. 'Just suck on this, go on, Susie, please.' His hand was on my crotch now, kneading gently, and his eyes were closed as he held his erection towards me like a gift.

I gaped at him through my one working eye, then stood up

and unzipped my jeans. I took them off, and my panties, and lay down on the bench. 'Go on, Jez. Get it over with.'

'Susie,' he was surprised, 'we can't do that. I'm married! Just suck it for me, Susie, oh pleeeeease,' he whined softly.

In that instant I saw my daddy standing by my bed, one hand on his crotch and one hand on mine. It was the first of many flashbacks. They started coming fast, and I felt like someone vomiting who can't stop. At first I thought I was going crazy; it took about a year for me to believe what I was seeing, and a few more to even begin to deal with it. But I'm dealing with it now.

Wheeze IV

Bo and Jeannie on one side with a swimming pool, and Maria and Virgilio on the other; you're sandwiched well there, Daddy. I know they look after you and make regular references to your saintly status. Everyone admired how well you looked after Mama for all those years. *That man's a saint*, they'd remark fondly, shaking their heads at the thought of it. Those with a bit more background into the situation suggested some trade-off was taking place. But Tildy was so scratchy, so claws-out all the time, it's hard not to sympathize and admire the patience with which you fed her, doctored her, wiped her top and her bottom. You dreamed of going home to Pennsylvania to see your kin, but wouldn't leave Mama, even for a weekend. Sacrifice became your *raison d'être*, your middle name. You wore it well.

One regret that nags at you is your yard. We never

lived anywhere but you had roses and tomatoes
planted all around the house. Some of your father's
blood there, I reckon. It was always sad to leave them,
often just blooming or ripening. I can't remember one
homegrown tomato ever making it to my mouth,
although I can't either say why this is. The plants
were certainly always there, and you spent enough
time fussing round them, Martini and cigarette in one
hand and clippers in the other. Now, with your
bersitis so painful it's impossible to even consider
digging or pruning, the beds are dry and cracked,
sparse weeds and little lizards the only resident
greenery. Still, you go outside so rarely now you
hardly see them. Gradually, all the people you used to
see regularly at their offices have reversed the tide;
they come to you with their pills and portable
machinery, they prod and poke and *tsk tsk tsk*, as if
you were deaf or something. You used to like getting
out . . . didn't you? I know all the ladies at the local
library adored you. You were a charmer, weren't you,
Daddy? To all but those closest to your heart. And
you even charmed us at times.

I know you'll be wandering in and out of this letter
like you wander from room to room. Can't seem to
settle on much of anything these days; can't even read a
book, for God's sake. TV works sometimes, but more
often than not you fall asleep, even when it's *Perry
Mason*. Take your time, Daddy. I'm taking mine.

What is this thing called family anyhow? Your daddy
wanted a farm and you planted roses. Your mama was
just a little bit crazy and you have moments of utter

separation from reality. My mama was furious and I suspect I'm riddled with fury, though I've never been able to connect with it the way the twins can. My daddy split himself in two and tore me up in the process. But there they are, all the photographs in place: Christmas, Easter, holidays and relocations, documented with religious care. We are mostly all smiles; only the odd crack shows, and only to those who might be looking for it. The perfect, modern, loving American family, smiling from the walls and scrapbooks like so many Cheshire cats.

Then there are the aunts, uncles, cousins, seen on rare or frequent occasions, sporting all manner of genetic doo-dahs that relate, or don't, to me. Who are we required to love? Are we required? Did you love me, Daddy? I can't figure it out. You used to write me little poems and send me heart-shaped sugary tributes. You let me wear your giant undershirts with the V-necks. You dried my hair by rubbing my bouncing head between your knees as I sat on the floor and you in your big soft chair.

These were good things, I guess.

What did your folks do for you, I wonder. Your mama scratched her face out of every picture that anyone had managed to take of her, even the one of her daughter's wedding. Couldn't bear her reflected image, either; it sent her wild. Disappointment, grief, a memory, or just plain neurosis, nobody ever knew. She was a sweet woman, from what I recall, and 'highly strung', according to common knowledge. Couldn't stand the curtains open, so you grew up in a dusky, trembly world, treading softly and whispering your 'Yes, Ma'ms' and 'No, Ma'ms'.

Some of that shadow stayed with you, clung to you, no matter how hard you tried to fly close to the sun. And you cast it about you like a suffocating shroud, choking those nearest while you seemed not to notice at all.

Attack

Bozo, Claire's cat, was sleeping on the kitchen windowsill. Joe and I were at the table, drinking tea. He'd had a bad few days, hardly sleeping at all. He'd just tried to catch a bus into town, but got to the bus stop and became so agitated he came home again. He was drumming his fingers on the table and muttering under his breath, I couldn't understand what.

'What about sleeping pills? I know it's not ideal, but you've got to do something.' Joe glared at me with hatred. I put my hand over his gently, to still it, but avoided his gaze. I had no idea what he might do. Joe was an erratic, moody man but I'd loved him for years, had played music and had a child with him. He was unusual, but that's what first attracted me to him, and I didn't want to lose him after all we'd been through together. He breathed out a little.

'Fucking bastards.' Joe's face was twisted into an appalled

grimace, as if he'd just swallowed a mouthful of turpentine. He was referring to his work mates.

'Have you tried talking to Trevor? You used to think he was OK.'

Joe stood up abruptly, knocking his cup on to the floor. 'That's just it. That's exactly it!' he bellowed. 'I don't need your fucking suggestions!'

'What do you want me to do?' I really didn't know.

'I want you to agree with me. To say, yeah, they all want lining up and shooting. They want their fucking heads blown off. Just *AGREE*.'

So what I thought was a logical response was fuel to the fire of his rage. He wanted a witness, not a counsellor.

'OK. When do we go get 'em?' I laughed stupidly, trying to bring him along. 'Now, or after dinner?'

Just then a couple of boys stopped outside the window, admiring the cat. They must have been about seven or eight years old. We could hear them talking. *Look, it's a cat. Is it alive? It's asleep.* One of the boys started tapping on the window, trying to wake Bozo and get her attention. Joe flipped. He staggered to the drawer and drew out the butcher knife. 'I'll get you, you little bastards. Come on.' He was waving the knife in circles, lunging at the window. The boys ran off, terrified.

My arms and legs had turned to rubber. 'Joe, it's OK, Joe, they're gone,' I whispered, glued to my seat, eyes following the slicing of the air around me. He stopped, dropping the knife with a clatter on to the linoleum. I managed to stand and take his arm in both of mine. I couldn't feel him at all. 'Let's go into the front room, OK?'

He followed me like a child. I sat him down in his chair and said, 'I'm going to go and run you a bath, all right? I think a bath might make you feel more relaxed.' Joe nodded and I went up the stairs on tiptoe, collapsing on to the landing at the top. I was gasping for breath. What was I going to do? What was he going to do next? I'd never seen him so bad. If I could get him into the bath, I'd have time to think. Claire wasn't due home from school for an hour.

Joe went for his bath and I phoned an acquaintance of his whom I knew was a psychiatric nurse. Joe didn't have many friends. The people he met for a drink occasionally were members of the Death Row Supporters group. But I'd met this guy, Mark, a few times, and he seemed nice. Plus, he worked in mental health. I whispered down the line, 'Hi, Mark, it's me, Susie, Joe's wife.'

'Hi!' He sounded surprised. 'Y'all right then?'

I stuttered, 'Yeah, I'm, well, no, Mark. I'm not. It's Joe. I think he's . . . he's . . . he's very uptight right now.'

'Oh yeah?' Joe always appeared very low key and self-contained. Mark would take some convincing. But I was desperate.

'He's just had a go at some little kids. With a knife. I'm scared.'

'A *knife*?'

'He didn't do anything, I mean, he didn't hurt them.' There was a pause at the other end. 'I think he just needs someone to talk to, Mark. Someone besides me. I don't know what else to do.'

'OK. I'll give him a ring sometime.'

'NOW, Mark. It's urgent. He needs to talk to someone now. Can you call him in thirty minutes? Arrange to meet? He's in the bath.'

Mark laughed. 'I'll call him in thirty minutes then. You sure you're OK?'

I was limp with relief. 'Thanks a lot. Really, thanks.'

'No problem.'

Joe came downstairs from his bath in a somewhat calmer mood, though he still had a weird look in his eye.

'Shall I start dinner?' I asked, and Joe nodded. He turned on the TV and the phone rang. I went into the kitchen and didn't hear the conversation, but Joe came in after a minute and said, 'That was Mark.'

'Oh?'

'We're going for a drink two weeks on Friday. The Dog and Partridge. Just him and me.'

I wanted to sob, or scream. Mark clearly thought I was the mad one. *Maybe*, I thought, *just maybe I am*.

That was the worst it got. Joe got better, so much better in fact that he ran off with Yvonne a year later.

Joe's leaving was like having a cast removed from a long-time broken leg: air and freedom, but you can't quite walk right. It reminded me of when Claire was small. As a baby, she looked like other babies her age, but weighed twice as much. *Iron constitution*, I thought at the time. Iron will soon to appear. I was forever nearly losing my grip on other babies, picking them up expecting more weight, and feeling them fly into the air like helium balloons. I was doing the same to myself now, lurching in all directions. I'd come adrift.

Kin

Great-grandma Thompson was the oldest person alive, I was convinced. I only got to meet her once. Her skin was dark and wrinkled all over, even on her fingers and ears. Her voice was like paper, rustly and fragile. She spoke in stories, about people called Orville and Beulah and Laverle and Boliver and Hyram and John Pope, plus lots of names that were just letters, like JI and JG and LJ and JC – a lot of Js for some reason. These were all my kin, and I was to remember that.

Tidmore Skeet was your grandfather's brother. He was married to Pansy, and they had a beautiful daughter, Rosella. She was so smart, she won a scholarship to study History at Rice University.

Her parents were proud and fiercely protective. Rosella had been delivered to them by angels (so they said) after Pansy had endured seven miscarriages. So they were careful about where she would live and whom she would meet. Pansy had a nervous disposition, and very nearly moved to Houston with her daughter, but Tid wouldn't hear of it. 'Give the girl some room,' he said, patting his wife's trembling hand. 'She'll be all right.'

They set her up in the household of friends of friends. Pansy and Tid lived in Beaumont. Tidmore was the Sheriff, and knew folks all over the state. He fixed it so that Rosella would be staying in Houston with the Howell family, one of the richest in Texas. They had a beautiful place, surrounded by five acres of land. There were horses and peacocks and Irish Setters, who all seemed to get along fine. Mitzi and Franklin Howell were philanthropists with a keen interest in the arts. Their six children were all grown and gone, but came to visit regularly with their own families and friends. The house was always humming with activity, and Rosella loved it there.

She quickly got into the habit of taking an early morning ride with Mitzi Howell. They would saddle up at dawn and gallop into the rising sun. Rosella had never felt so grown up and alive. When Mitzi twisted her ankle on a break in the sidewalk downtown, Rosella rode out on her own.

She hadn't spoken much to Pedro, the stable man. She had noticed his black eyes and ease with the animals, his sensitivity, his powerful build. He was tall for a Mexican, Rosella thought, but then she didn't know many Mexicans. She'd mainly seen them bent over in the fields.

They got friendly. Pedro was twenty-two years old, from Matamoros. His family were all still in Mexico, and he sent them most of his weekly wages. He missed his six sisters terribly. Rosella was moved, in more ways than one.

One morning Franklin walked Rosella to the stables. He didn't like her riding on her own, even though her skills as a horsewoman had improved dramatically since she'd moved to Houston. There were snakes that could cause a horse to shy and buck, and there were *sometimes alligators in Buffalo Bayou, which ran along the eastern edge of the grounds. Horses and alligators didn't mix.*

'Morning, Pedro,' Franklin waved. 'How's your mama and the kiddies?'

'She's just fine, Mr Howell. How are you?'

'Off to Dallas this morning. I want you to do something for me, if you will.'

'Of course,' Pedro nodded.

'Will you ride with Miss Rosella here? I'd feel better if she had some company.'

'Sure I will. I'll take Yankee out. He could use a run.' Pedro paused. 'You want me to go every day?' He glanced at Rosella, who was trying to hide her delight by examining her boots.

'If you don't mind.' Franklin was a liberal man, popular with his staff. He bid them both goodbye and strode off.

The two became inseparable. Rosella would rush to classes and back again. She started riding in the evenings too. They were falling in love. They told no one. They couldn't. Rosella knew her mama and daddy would have a fit. A Mexican? Impossible. But there was nothing she could do about it. And every time they dismounted and lay on the mossy banks of the bayou, it was getting harder to stand up again.

'This is our world,' they would tell each other, Spanish moss hanging over their heads, cottonmouths swimming by, until one day in the unbearable heat of their passion Pedro stood and said, 'NO, cara mia. THE WORLD is our world. Marry me.'

They ran off and did it. When Tid and Pansy found out they were mortified.

'No longer a child of mine,' and so on. 'Never darken our door,' with the emphasis on DARK. Rosella thought her heart would break. But it was her body that did.

They were living in a house off Fuqua, small and cramped but a happy house because it contained them both. The Howells helped them out some, but felt conflicted in doing so. Liberal in those days had a long way to go.

Rosella fell pregnant and left college. Pedro was working for the city parks, not a bad wage. They couldn't believe their luck, and now a child to cement their union and maybe bring Tidmore and Pansy around.

Rosella went into labour in her thirty-seventh week. Something was wrong. She lost a lot of blood and died giving birth to a five-pound girl. They never did find out what killed her. Women in those days just died sometimes. Pedro could barely breathe for grief. He named his daughter Rosella Maria, and went with her to Beaumont, hoping for a reconciliation.

Pansy and Tid said, 'We'll raise this child and give her all she could want. But only if you stay away from here for ever. Understand?'

Pedro had no family to help with looking after the baby. He had to work, to send money to his folks in Matamoros, and to stay alive. He wanted to give his daughter security and comfort, but it wasn't his to offer. So he handed her over. He never saw Rosella Maria again.

No one knows what became of him. Some say he stayed around Beaumont, keeping track of baby Rosella's progress, spying on her from across streets and behind trees. But with Tid so powerful, it doesn't seem likely.

He never should have touched her, that's the truth.

Bubba

His first knife was a rubber one that he had gotten for his fifth birthday. He had charged around all day threatening to scalp everyone he came across, whooping and stomping and howling like a dog.

His next knife, a Swiss Army multi-purpose variety, was for Boy Scout activities: camping, fishing, and helping old ladies across the street. You never knew when it might come in handy.

Bubba became a serious collector of knives after he left college, of Bowies and switchblades and all manner of sheath knives and penknives from all over the world. Then, in the space of five years, he married, divorced, and moved back to Texas. There it was guns. He'd had a .22 since he was twelve, and a Remington 700 for deer hunting. We'd all been taught to shoot tin cans, even me. But Bubba became besotted with the particular beauty of handguns in his thirties.

Bubba became a connoisseur. He joined the NRA and subscribed to *Guns and Ammo* and *Combat Handguns* and *Guns and Weapons for Law Enforcement* and more. The twins still shoot to hunt sometimes, but have developed a preference for bows and arrows. A weapon, to them, is merely a way to eat well. Bubba keeps a loaded gun in every room of his house, in his car's glove compartment, and on his person, except at work.

He still doesn't feel safe.

Bubba lives with his second wife Jolene in the Montrose district of Houston. This is the gay neighbourhood, full of art galleries, junk shops and furnishers of sado-masochistic clothing and accoutrements. Bubba is always careful to point out to strangers that he lives in Montrose '. . . *with my wife.*'

Bubba has a good job, which he likes a lot. He lives 'one day at a time' except for the rare periods when he deliberately falls off the wagon. He's been an alcoholic since he was twenty-one, and a recovering alcoholic since he was thirty-six. Fifteen years of a spiral into hell, including car wrecks, DTs, blackouts, a brief but eventful marriage and an only son. Jolene helps to keep him level. She can spit fire when she needs to.

'You're so stupid you couldn't pour piss out of a boot if the directions were written on the bottom. You're so fulla shit your eyes are brown.' Jolene has a way with words.

Every weekend Bubba and Jolene visit Daddy. Jolene hasn't seen her dad since she was six, and doesn't want to either. He's a con man and a gambler who left them all in the shit when he went. So she has a lot of time for Daddy. Tildy was another story. When Tildy was alive Jolene usually found some excuse not to go on these weekly visits. Tildy was a pain in the ass, didn't have a sweet word for anybody as far as Jolene could see. Claws out all the time. But with Tildy dead and buried, Jolene looks forward to going.

One weekend in December – it was cold by Houston standards, near freezing with snow in the air – they arrived to find Daddy in a state. He kept a flashlight in every drawer in every room, and was always losing track of one or the other of them. Daddy never used the overhead lights at night, just wandered the hallway with his flashlight, checking the locks and the thermostat over and over again.

The previous night he had somehow lost every one of his flashlights, so he'd dialled 911 and demanded that they bring him a replacement. They'd told him no, that wasn't their job, he could go and buy one in the morning. Daddy was furious, fidgeted and muttered and cursed for an hour or so, and then called again. Miss G warned him, *Mr E, I don't think you better do that*, but he did. He told her, *I've served my country all my life and if my country can't provide me with a Goddamn flashlight I don't know what the world's coming to.* This time he was told that if he phoned once more he would be fined for wasting their time.

He was still fuming when Bubba and Jolene arrived. Bubba tried to explain to Daddy that the emergency services couldn't be doing stuff like that, but Daddy was adamant. This was when Bubba realized that Daddy was, in fact, losing it.

Jolene managed to cheer Daddy up some with her wisecracks and the chocolate-marshmallow fudge she'd made and brought especially for him. They found the flashlights all together in the sidetable drawer in the mostly unused back bedroom. How they got there nobody could say, but at least Daddy had them again, and he went around putting each one in its place, much like Bubba did with his guns, checking and rechecking.

The Ring

Tildy was dying, but believed firmly that she was dead already and had been for a long time. What else could explain the barrenness of her soul, the absence of any warmth or affection for anything or anyone, even her own children and grandchildren? All they did was want from her, a sticky smothering want that had gradually grown in her this seething, infuriated blank, like a whiteout in a blizzard, a blizzard of howling disregard. It was eating her up.

She could vaguely remember feeling more, but that was before she'd embarked on the numbing journey of matrimony and its attendant squalor and disappointment. Miss Tildy had been something of a wild child, always pushing the boundaries, sneaking under the flap of the circus tent just to see if she could do it, driving her father's Model T so fast down Main Street that it took a full week to get the dust out of the Five & Dime, the door of which happened to be open as she passed. She would stand back sweet and sassy after one of these escapades, hands on her slender hips and a glow of satisfaction in her bright brown eyes, daring anyone to challenge her behaviour, and knowing no one would. Naughty but nice, everyone agreed, and certainly virginal until her honeymoon. A charmer who held out for the tallest, handsomest stranger despite the many and varied pleas for her hand. Saying no was one of her favourite things, the pleasure of holding someone else's heart in your hand and then setting it gently, gently down and walking away. Thrilling.

Now she was reduced to rare syllables of peace interrupted by complex sentences of torment. Daddy even had to put her on the potty, wipe her bottom like she was a child. He expected gratitude, but he wasn't going to get it, oh no. He'd get what he deserved, and no more. She did love him, she supposed, or had at one time. It was more a memory than anything else, and didn't engage her blood or flesh. But then, she was dead, so how could it? Real feelings were just memories, which seemed a great distance from her and blurred; shapeless as the food she had to force down at Daddy's insistence. Yuk. This couldn't go on; she'd had enough. If that damn Frank Gordon could escape the conscious world, so could she. She'd even go a step further; Tildy wouldn't lie around hooked up to tubes and wires and whatall while people stood and gawped. Oh, no.

Tildy needed to prepare. She was determined to leave a statement behind, something solid, a message from the grave. If there were such a thing as an afterlife, she'd be there, hanging in the ether, watching – ohhh, delight. She'd feel this for sure, get something back from the death she'd been living for too long.

Tildy saw me as a particularly cloying, wimpish thing. No backbone. How Tildy had ever managed to produce such a walking failure of spirit she couldn't figure; must be Daddy's genetic influence. I had nearly driven her crazy on more than one occasion, with my *I love you, Mama*s and *I miss you, Mama*s. Pathetic. I needed reminding of how badly I'd let my mother down.

When we kids were small, Tildy had promised us each a personal keepsake when she died. We'd looked at her with horrified faces: *But, Mama, you're not ever going to die!* Funny, how terrified we'd been. She'd told us that, yes, she would indeed die, and when she did, Bubba would have her father's pocket watch, I would have the jade ring, and the twins could have her collection of Navajo turquoise and silver. But I had pissed her off one too many times. She needed to teach me a lesson.

Daddy had put her to bed, as usual, at ten. Her little TV was on to cover any sound Daddy might hear and check on. His room was down the hall, and he was probably in his bathroom brushing his teeth anyway. She sat up on the edge of the bed and switched on the lamp, then reached for her jewellery box. She opened it quietly and removed the jade ring, then put the box back and leaned against her pillows, putting her legs under the covers again but leaving the light on. She contemplated the ring, and a memory came back to her with such a rush that her hair bristled.

One night years ago, when she was reading in bed late at night, she'd heard me call her, loudly: *MAMA!* Only I was in college at the time, 500 miles away. She'd thought she was imagining things and gone back to her book, when she'd heard it again, even louder. She'd put her book down and taken off her glasses, listening intently, and annoyed, for sounds of an unexpected arrival for a visit, or something like that. Silence. Tildy was pretty sure there was no one downstairs, so she told herself she'd read her book, but if she heard me again she'd go down and take a look. It didn't happen again. I happened to phone the following weekend, and when I heard my mother's story I was shocked. On the night in question I had been heard by my roommate to cry out for my mother twice in my sleep. The roommate had been so disturbed by the sound of these cries that she'd determined to wake me up if it happened a third time, but it didn't. Weird. Of course, I had wanted to make too much of it, gushing on about this indication of our 'psychic connectedness', our closeness in spite of the miles and the fact that we'd never gotten along very well to begin with. We'd always clashed. Tildy had refused to discuss it again, so that solved that.

This vivid remembering diverted her from her course, but she shook herself out of it, shook me out of her mind and closed her eyes for a moment to refocus. The ring was warm now in her hand. She took the glass of water Daddy always left on the bedside table in her other hand. She popped the ring into her mouth and drank quickly; it was down in the first gulp, but she finished the glass to be sure. It was easy, because it was right. Then, she took the pack of Camels she had hidden at the back of her bedside table drawer and shook one out. She lit it and smoked it, then lit another and another until half the pack was empty. Tildy switched off the light and laid back, grinning like she hadn't done in years, and her loose and sagging spirit lifted for that moment; there was even a hint of the old charm about her, a sparkle in her eyes. She was asleep in minutes, dreaming of hearts and hearts and hearts at her feet.

Daddy found her dead the next morning when he took her orange juice in. She was lying on her back, eyes wide open and mouth closed in the softest of smiles.

New Music

When I left The Goat and Whistle, I figured it was about time I did something with my education. I decided to become a teacher. It would fit in well with Claire's requirements, and it would be a chance to go back to school and see if the old brain would kick in and hack it. I would need a teaching qualification, which would take a year, and then I'd go forth and be a tender of little minds and souls, all heart and harmony and passionate conviction. I would teach music. I would really teach the world to sing, or at least this little English corner of it. I would be avocationally charged and committed, and, at last, one of the good guys.

Joe didn't like it. He had gotten used to being the winner in all respects – bread, marathons and the moral high ground. I was so used to this definition of the world that at first it seemed impossible to shift. I'd flunk out, fail my teaching practices, be pilloried by teachers and pupils alike. But I made it through the course, and got a job to boot. Things were looking up.

I was terrified on my first day. It was a tough school with an ex-hippy headteacher who wore sandals and hugged all and sundry (within legal limits). He played the guitar and sang 'Give Peace a Chance' in assemblies. I was often asked what schools were like in the USA, but I couldn't remember a thing, not a favourite teacher or subject or worst moment or anything at all. People eyed me strangely when I gave this response, so I took to saying 'Oh, about the same really. Different exam system. You know.' Which seemed more acceptable.

What scared me most was standing in front of thirty kids and asking for their attention. I'd think, *Why on earth should they listen to me? What do I know?* But I settled in, pushing this question to the back of my mind, and it mostly worked. I even enjoyed it, a lot of the time. But there were exceptions.

A rough and ready Year Nine group caused me a lot of trouble that first year. There were some real characters: Jason Stoops, who was fond of getting his weenie out under the table, Sabrina Evans, who could sing like Bessie Smith but couldn't sit still, and Kelly Harper, who beat other kids up with terrifying precision and regularity, among others. They were fascinating, and I was largely inclined to just sit back and watch them bubble away, but this was not really possible. For one thing, they'd have had the musical keyboards in pieces in about one red hot minute; for another, I'd have lost my job.

So, I did my best to impart some musical skills to this rag-tag lot, and some days it worked. Most of them had managed to learn 'Why Do Fools Fall in Love', both playing and singing along in harmony. The bottom end got very carried away with their *um-badada*s, but that was OK. It was their very success that caused the whole thing to fall apart one day.

They'd just finished a rousing and near-perfect rendition of the song. Jason's penis was in his pants and Sabrina had outdone herself. I'd suggested to the group that they perform it in assembly. All agreed except Sabrina, who felt she should be paid for a public performance. The rest cottoned on pretty quickly to this idea. *We could take a collection, Miss! Yeah, Miss, or Sir could pay us. Come on, Miss!* I started to explain that this was an educational act rather than a vocational one when Kelly turned around to Sabrina and said, *Shut your fucking mouth. Think you're so cool.* She punched Sabrina solidly in the mouth and blood was all at once everywhere. Sabrina fell off of her chair in shock. Kelly stood up, waving her fists at the room. *Anyone else? Huh?*

I said to Marie Plant, sitting nearest the door, *Go and get Mr Antony.* He was the Deputy in charge of discipline. Then I said to Kelly, *Pack your bag, kiddo, you're going.* Kelly glared at me. She gathered her things, marched to the door, opened it, then turned back to the class. She pointed her finger at me and screamed *FUCKING WHORE!!!!* and slammed the door as hard as she could.

There were gasps all around and then at least five seconds of silence (a record) before the kids gathered round me, soothing and patting me, saying, *That wasn't very nice, Miss. She's a silly cow, Miss. She's stupid, her.* I wanted to throw my arms around all of them, but I was trying not to cry. All I could think was, *How does SHE know? How does she KNOW?* But, of course, she didn't. Not really. At least I hoped not.

We eventually performed the song in assembly, to schoolwide acclaim. The applause turned out to be enough for

Sabrina. She spent a lot of that lunchtime signing autographs for Year Seven kids, with Kelly as her bodyguard. It's funny how things turn out sometimes. Isn't it?

And so, I became a semi-permanent fixture at that place, along with the peeling paint and dusty corridors, along with the constant influx and departure of kids and kids and kids. I had few friends in the staffroom. I thought it was better that way. My history is far too suspect to share, and besides, there are the scars, which I don't like to talk about. What I loved about teaching was that there was always a small person with a question to ask, a question I could usually answer with the truth.

Claim

1:30 pm Mr E claim + sleeping.
1:42 pm Mr E talking to Bubba.
1:54 pm Bubba left.
2:00 pm Mr E asleep + coughing.
2:30 pm Mr E resless.
3:00 pm Mr E claim.
4:00 pm Mr E resless.
4:30 pm Mr E claim.
5:00 pm Mr E resless.
5:30 pm Mr E claim.
6:00 pm Mr E eating pork chopp and aplesauce.

And so on. Miss Posetta G's spelling was erratic (she meant to write *calm*), but her heart was in the right place. Figuratively speaking, of course, seeing as how her figure hadn't been in the right place since the car crash in '65. It had twisted her spine so badly they hadn't thought she'd survive. But she did, with God, Billy and her mother by her side. Mornings were toughest; getting out of bed was like cracking an old pecan, one broken sliver of meat after another. She'd had to give up nursing and the spunky life and save dressing up for church. With only one working arm and a leg like a lock-picker's coathanger, she could still cut a mean and mighty dash through the gravestones. And her cut-glass smile still made the parson sweat.

Billy had taken good care of her until he died of diabetes and carelessness in '82. She still missed him violently at times, and not just because making ends meet had put her in this babysitter's hell. He was her man, and there'd be no other. Oh, a few had started making courting noises, but they had their eyes on her bought-and-paid-for house and her fried chicken. She was just fine with her seven nieces for company.

This job, though. Agency work: Loving Live-Ins. Coming into folks' houses, tending the old and near-dead like children, taking their tantrums and orders like the slave she thought she'd never be. It made her belly boil sometimes, but she needed the cash. Mr E wasn't too bad, and Bubba his son was a sweetie. Miss G loved to cook for him on Saturdays, and he liked it too. He sure did look after his daddy.

Something funny was going on though, and had been for a while. These letters had started coming, about one a week, from England. Miss G knew he had a daughter overseas, and thought they were probably from her. He never spoke much about that one, or the twins either, even though their photographs lined the walls with Bubba's. Bubba was his favourite, Posetta guessed. You weren't supposed to have favourites but most parents did in her experience. She knew she was her mother's most adored, and so did her brothers. Nobody seemed to mind.

It was Mr E's reaction to these letters that was odd. He'd get real agitated and roam the house even more than usual. When she asked him what the matter was he'd just sigh his hound-dog sigh and mutter under his breath, something about hell and damnation and why can't she just leave me alone.

It seemed to Posetta that white folks didn't have much family feeling. They hung pictures of their kids up so everyone could see they'd done the right thing. But there was little connection between them. Seemed like parents couldn't wait to get their kids off their hands, with the result being the fact that they ended up alone and lonely in old age. Then it was people like Posetta who picked up the pieces, and endured the anger and bitterness she came across so frequently in this job.

7:00 pm Mr E finished 1/2 pork chopp and all aplesauce with some potatoes.
8:00 pm Mr E re-reading leters, geting adgitated and mutering. Won't talk about it.
10:00 pm Mr E takes leters to bed.

When Aliens Took the Wind from His Sails

Joe's thirty-sixth year came and went, but he decided to stick around. We didn't talk about it. I was afraid to bring it up in case he'd just forgotten; I didn't want to remind him.

We didn't talk about a lot of things. But Joe did tell me about Yvonne one August, and in September he was gone, leaving Claire and me shattered and in shock. It shouldn't have come as such a surprise, but it did. I was used to Joe. But being used to someone is no guarantee they'll always be there. Especially if they meet someone as lovely as Yvonne.

This is how I imagine Joe's life now. I have to imagine, because his hostility towards me increases as every day goes by, and he hasn't spoken to me for five years. But I hear from Claire that he has re-established contact with his parents, and sees them regularly. A shift of focus, I guess. I can see him:

Bitch, he thinks.

Stupid bitch.

Stupid cunting fucking hellish bitch.

That feels better. He breathes out slowly and brings the bicycle on to the level with ease. The fear leaves his heart racing but slightly now, not like the pounding pressure of freefall, of any little bump in the road could throw you so far you'd never come back. He has to do it, he tells himself, has to. No choice. Has daily to take that risk, for his sake and for Yvonne's.

Joe is a dresser in navy blues and greys and blacks. He favours dark jeans and plain sweatshirts, and owns only one suit, which he bought from Oxfam for his uncle's funeral. His usual air of scruffiness is borne of several factors. For one thing, he grew too fast. His skin could never quite keep up with his bones, so he acquired a look, by the time he reached his final six foot one, of a badly wrapped package. For another, he always had a lot to hide, and he didn't want to stick out too much in company. But when he's on his bike, he becomes the cock he is, an exotic display of the brightest, gaudiest hues, luminescent and proud of it. The stretch of fluorescent lycra against his thigh and he's transported. He even likes his helmet. There are a lot of cyclists who resent this invaluable bit of gear; they'd rather feel the wind in their hair and risk permanent brain damage. Joe's hair, or rather the gradual loss of it, had led him at several points in his life to try wearing a hat, but he never could pull it off. So his helmet is a source of great pride to him, and he wears it with some style, though for obvious reasons a rakish angle is not a possibility.

About a year after taking up cycling, when we were still together, Joe had started shaving his legs. It is, after all, rec-ommended for racers to do so; a nasty fall and you've got both gravel and hairs to extricate from the damaged flesh. He'd found it kind of weird at first, comparing favoured methods with his daughter. She'd laughed about it, but she'd understood. I don't shave my legs, and found the whole thing wildly comical.

Bitch, he thinks, I can hear it in my head. *Fucking cunt. Good riddance.*

He takes the bike to the side of the road and gets off, taking the water bottle out of its holder. Sitting on a rock, he looks out over the moors. He loves it out there, the space, the view unbroken by anything, or anyone, but the next steep hill. A fine drizzle starts to come down, so he wipes his glasses, replaces the bottle and saddles up for the home run. He feels happy with his life, and about time too. He barely managed to survive eighteen years of hell, a marriage that never should have happened and that very nearly did him in. He'd never realized how impossible it would turn out to be living with a foreigner. Sure, it was interesting at first. And it had got him finally away from his mother. But, looking back, it was clear that their differences were too great, had always been too great to make it work. He'd very nearly gone under with the strain of it all: a wife at once frigid and over-heated, a non-stop talker with, ultimately, nothing to say to him.

Meeting Yvonne was what saved him. Everything became clear in an instant, it was like one of those visions you read about that change people's lives for ever. Yvonne had given him his life back.

He is coming into town now, so he'd better keep his eye on the road. He hates this town almost as much as he does the people in it, and he is sure that more than one of the dickheads would drive right at him, given the chance. He has to stay vigilant. Yvonne knows. Every one of her bloody husbands had been a psychopath, and the fact that they all got custody just served to prove how devious they were. The kids are all as warped as their fathers anyway. Yvonne is better out of it, and just with him. Together they have all they need.

He gets home and puts on his slippers, then settles himself in front of the telly with a cup of tea. The new carpet means no shoes in the lounge – Yvonne is adamant about this. He loves that about her. The new wallpaper looks good too, and the furniture. Just right, finally. He'd finally gotten his life just right. Yvonne will get home at about five fifteen; that gives him nearly an hour until he has to change clothes. He likes to keep his cycling gear on for as long as possible when he is alone.

He stares at the telly but his mind wanders. He is thinking about the one incident he ever told me about concerning his parents: his mother, and the time she'd made him take his new guitar back to the shop. She'd been keeping track of his money, which he kept in a tin by his bed, and when she'd realized that £30 was missing she went mad. *Bloody nerve*, Joe thinks, *considering I was twenty-two at the time.* Thing is, he hadn't even had the bottle to bring the guitar home; he'd known his parents wouldn't approve, so he'd taken it round to a friend's house. Still, he'd never imagined for a minute that she'd count his dosh. The humiliation when he'd collected it from his friend wasn't anything compared to what he'd had to go through in the shop. They'd thought he was a pillock. *Bastards.*

He shakes himself out of this memory and focuses his mind

on his new acquisitions: a dobro, a 60s lap steel and a mountain bike. *Good thing the cunt paid up*, he thinks. *£4,500 – not much of a payoff for eighteen years of hell. But at least I've got something to show for it. All she's got is an old house in serious need of repair.* This thought causes the corners of his mouth to turn up, ever so slightly. He's been absently stroking his satin smooth shin, and now a soft shudder goes through him. He checks his watch; thirty minutes more until Yvonne gets home. Good.

Kemah Shrimps

It was Claire's eighteenth birthday. I'd organized a big party in a hired room. Everybody would arrive at eight. There'd be a DJ and a bar. At eleven the adults would come back to my house and eat, and the teenagers would stay at the party.

I was nervous because Joe would be there. He'd been living with Yvonne for just over a year, and his hostility towards me was growing rather than diminishing, as you might expect. He could glare holes in the ozone, that man, and it felt like he was trying to glare a hole in me whenever our paths crossed. 'He's ill-wishing you,' my friend Sandra said. 'Burn a purple candle and say a prayer. Or, close your eyes and create a circle of light around him and say, "Let all bad thoughts and feelings return to their source."' Sandra was a herbalist and healer. She'd performed many a ritual in my back garden, including officiating at the ceremonial burying of my uterus under a medlar tree.

'I gave him a hard time, Sandra. It wasn't easy being married to me.'

'Yeah, you did. But you've both got to get on with it now. He's bullying you, and you're letting him do it.'

I sighed, nodding at my friend. I wasn't looking forward to spending an evening in the same room as Joe.

Things kicked off OK. The room was the lounge bar of a big nightclub. It was perfect, with a smallish dance floor and comfortable seats. The DJ was lively and funny, and played a lot of sixties stuff for the older generation. I danced like a dervish, looking everywhere but at Joe, who stayed glowering at the bar. I drank too much, and got pretty friendly with our new neighbour, Pete, who was twenty years younger than me and had a PhD in History. He was also heavily involved in re-enacting famous medieval battles. He belonged to a group who did this regularly, had all the weapons and gear. An unusual man.

Claire saw that I was getting wobbly, and took me aside. 'Don't get totally drunk, please, Mum. Remember Katie and Emma are coming back to stay.'

'I won't, sweetie, don't worry. I'm just kind of nervous,' I slurred, leaning on the wall. Claire saw it was too late.

'I just get so nervous, baby, you know what I'm like.'

'Yeah. I know.'

I thought I was 'coping', but Claire saw it differently.

Claire asked the DJ to make an announcement ordering all elders home, so we piled out and got on buses. I'd made a pot of chilli and salads and there was plenty of bread and cheese. We ate, and people drifted off until just Pete and I were left. We were dancing a slobbery slow dance when the girls came home and went up to Claire's room. I thought they were asleep when I took my knickers off and lay down with Pete on the couch. They weren't.

We were right in the middle of a drunken fuck when Claire came in the room. She went mad. Pete ran off to his house and Claire started kicking me. She didn't stop until her anger was used up. I was black and blue.

The next morning we didn't speak until the phone rang. It was my father, telling me that Tildy was dead. I had this picture in my mind of my mother orchestrating the whole affair, her spirit riding above us, her bitter cackle: *See? I told you you're no good. Little whore.* But I guess that would be too easy.

I flew to Houston the next day, a Thursday. The funeral was to be held on Saturday morning. I hadn't been home in years, hadn't seen Daddy or the twins or the aunts and uncles, so it shocked me how they had aged. I had too. Bubba comes to Europe on business most years, so we'd kept up.

I looked around me as we entered the funeral parlour. This is the first, I thought, the first funeral of this generation. It was an open coffin, and Mama had more make-up on than she ever wore in life. It stunk, and combined with the scent of two dozen roses in a spray nearby, it made me sick to my stomach. I was reeling, not just with nausea, but with an overwhelming violence I felt as I looked down on my mother. I wanted to pummel her chest. I wanted to beat her up.

I started bawling, clutching my fists over my eyes so as not to strike my mother's gaudy corpse. Aunt Gracie came up and cuddled me. 'You're going to miss your mama, aren't you, Susie?'

I wanted to scream, 'I've always missed my mama! Every

day of my life I've missed my mama!' But Gracie wouldn't have understood.

The next day we went to Kemah, Daddy, Bubba and Jolene, the twins and I, and got twenty pounds of shrimp fresh off the boat. I boiled them up and melted butter while Bubba ran out to Grandy's for some french fries. Mama used to make the french fries herself, but hadn't in recent years, due to her illness, so Daddy had developed a Grandy's habit. We sat peeling shrimps and dipping them in bowls of butter, sucking our fingers and wiping our chins between mouthfuls. It had been a long time since we'd all sat down together. The only thing we could think to talk about was would Daddy be OK? He could finally get to spend time with his remaining brother and sister in Pennsylvania. He was non-committal, just nodded and shook his head when required. There was a lot I wanted to say, but it wasn't the right time, and I was leaving the next day. I would write to him instead.

Later, we started going through Tildy's things, distributing clothes and belts and hats and bags and shoes and scarves to various aunts and cousins and to the Goodwill. When we got to the jewellery, I looked for Mama's jade ring, which she had promised me when I was a child, but it wasn't there. Daddy said, 'I'm sure it was here.' He was the one who dressed Tildy every morning, and put her jewellery on and took it off. Grandpa's pocketwatch was there for Bubba, and the turquoise and silver for the twins, and everything else, but no jade ring. I felt ridiculously awful about this. It felt like the one promise my mother had ever made me she didn't keep.

Bubba drove me to the airport the following evening. I cried all the way there, choking sobs, and all the way home to

Claire. Bubba had said, 'What are you crying for? She was a bitch, and once a bitch, always a bitch. She's not worth crying for.' But I felt smothered by grief. My heart felt chopped in half. I felt like something was lodged in my throat, and I could hardly breathe.

Wheeze V

Posetta told Bubba that my letters are upsetting you,
Daddy. But Bubba knows I'm writing, and he knows
why. He doesn't want to get involved, but I have his
approval. We're all in it together anyway, because we
all lived it together, even though not one of us would
describe it the same.

This is the last letter I'm going to write. I want some
response this time, Daddy, so I'm going to call you two
weeks after I've mailed it. You're going to have to think
of something to say.

You'll be sitting at the kitchen table now, smoking
and drinking your two fingers of coffee. You won't
want to read on; you'll be terrified of what's about to
come. You'll have almost gotten used to the arrival of
these missives, even look forward to them in a
masochistic kind of way, the churning guts and quaking

hands. After all, it was always there waiting to happen, and at least that particular edginess is gone now.

Damn it to hell, I'm freezing, you'll think, and wander into the hallway to fiddle with the thermostat. Miss Posetta might be reading in the back room, her room now. She'll hear you coming and say, *Now, Mr E, we don't need no heating on, it's ninety degrees outside.*

Don't tell me what I can and can't do in my own house, you'll mutter, *damnation*. But you'll leave it and head back to the table, picking up a toothpick as you pass the coffee table. It hurts when you bend down; you'll wince slightly, but won't bother to put on the brace you're supposed to wear for the compression fractures in two of your vertebrae. It's uncomfortable, and the doctor can go to hell. You'll sit down again and pick your teeth for a minute, take a swig of coffee, and read on.

Your childhood had its weirdnesses, but I don't think that it left big bleeding wounds. Of course, something may have happened to you, a dark secret still untold. These things happen all the time, as we know. But I'm inclined to think it was the sense of dislocation left by the war, and the military career, and the gin that did you in.

Tildy, too. Oh I ache when I think of my beautiful mama, feisty, spunky little Tildy who burned herself up with bitterness and could see no other relief but the bottle. I spent so much heart on her, trying to clutch at her skirts and be good, but she couldn't see anything for seeing so much red. One of my many shrinks told me I was stuck on Mama because she was stuck on me; I looked so much like her, everyone said, and she could never separate completely from her only girl. Her self-hatred became my self-hatred: her maternal gift, along with her big brown eyes.

You'll be getting weepy with all this talk of Tildy. I know you miss her, Daddy; all those years together make for strong bonding, and you did take good care of her in the end. You'll pull a Kleenex from the box that's always on the counter behind the table, next to the napkin holder and the cinnamon shaker. You love cinnamon on your applesauce, and we all learned to love it too, though eating applesauce is not a habit I've carried into my adult life. It just never occurs to me to buy it. You'll take off your glasses and wipe your eyes and blow your nose, then let out a juddery sigh.

Bubba tells me that Miss Posetta has found you a few times wandering the hallway at night with your flashlight, looking for Mama. *Where's Mother? Where is she?* you'll ask as she guides you back to bed, explaining that Tildy died a year ago, it was a beautiful funeral, Cousin Billy led the service – all the things Bubba told her to say. It must be hard to bear, knowing that sometimes you lose the plot altogether, especially for a man so rigorous in his routines and habits.

Sometimes I wish I'd never remembered anything. But a subconscious search was in operation, and once I had found the perfect combination of fists and fornication, the floodgates opened and I had to swim with the current, or go down. Your violence, Daddy, is something I haven't touched on yet. It came in two packages: the tantrum, when you lashed out like a rodeo bullwhipper at whomever you could reach, and

the deliberate, when you took the errant one into
his/her bedroom, made him/her lean over the bed with
his/her pants down, slowly removed your belt from its
loops and set about the punishment, counting the
strokes and saying *This hurts me more than it hurts you.*
Yes, Daddy, I know it's corny, but you always said that.
It gives me the shivers just writing it down.

You didn't beat us often, or with any kind of
regularity. It was impossible to tell what would set you
off, so Bubba, the twins and I were pretty careful
around you, especially weekday evenings when you'd
been at work and it took three dry Martinis to take the
edge off of your day and enable you to face dinner. You
were often worse when Tildy was on a bender,
especially when we were smaller. You made us promise
never to tell a soul about Mama's drinking, and we
didn't, which made life tough when you were away and
there was no food, or Mama hurt herself, which
happened quite frequently. Bubba took charge, he
looked after all of us, a big job for a little boy. It took
its toll on him, too. But he's fine now, or as fine as he
can be. As you know.

You'll be thinking, *Why is she telling me what I already
know? What is the point of all this?* But the truth is, I
don't know what you know. I think there is such a deep
divide between your waking sense of reality and the
dark corridors of your soul that the two rarely meet.
You are just as split as I am.

Don't get me wrong, Daddy; I'm not letting you off
the hook here. Somewhere inside you the knowledge
exists that you hurt me, and the rest of us, badly. And

you've suffered for it, I know. Pain begets pain begets pain. We've had enough, haven't we? It's time to stop. I'm going to do the most radical thing I can think of to put an end to all this pain.

I'm coming to see you.

The Moon

On the night of the day Claire left home the moon was as fat and wide and white as one of Tildy's best dinner plates, with the same fool's gold edging: magical, reminiscent and begging for blood. I had thought I was fine, having spent the previous day moving furniture and packing bags. We got pizza and played cribbage until three am. Claire beat me four times in a row! I remember when I used to let her win. We were both still sleepy when I dropped her off the next morning, and I wasn't expecting to weep, but I did.

'I . . . this is hard for me,' I spluttered, taken by surprise.

'Aw, Mum, you'll be OK.' Claire hugged me and patted my back at the same time, just as I had done a thousand years ago when she was small and hurt. 'I'll call you later, all right?'

'I'm going to Franny's for dinner. We're going to practise our cackling and bay at the moon.'

Claire laughed. 'You lot ought to be tagged. You're

dangerous.' She loosened her hold. 'I'll ring you in the morning then.'

She's so ENGLISH, I thought. My flesh and blood, and so English. As I drove back to my house I couldn't stop wondering, how did I get here? What am I doing here? Am I redundant now the fledgling is airborne? Should I just go home? But where the hell is that?

When I walked into my house and shut the door it rang hollow and forlorn. This was it. This was me, alone. Would I stay lucid, or would I increasingly talk to myself, mutter mutter muttering the shopping lists and issues of the day? Talking back to the television?

Franny and Sandra: these were my buddies, my cronehood companions. We had looked after each other's mortal souls for years, engaging in the kind of alchemy that turns heartache into survival, over and over again. We held each other's hands and heads and histories, while lovers came and went, children grew and moved, jobs and houses changed. We held rituals at important moments. One of the funniest was when I had a hysterectomy.

I was just about to turn forty. The doctor wasn't sure what was there, but she knew something was. We examined it together on the ultrasound screen. I thought of it as my Foreign Body, my UFO. I didn't like the idea of losing my innards to an alien invader. A thought occurred to me:

'Can I have it when you've taken it out?'

Dr Storey looked alarmed.

'Not the THING, my uterus I mean. Can I take it home?'

'Well, I've had quite a few requests for placentas recently but never for a womb. What are you planning to do with it?'

The idea was forming as I answered. 'I'll plant it in my

garden with a tree or something on top. That way I'll still have a womb, only in a different place.'

The doctor laughed, shaking her head. 'I'll see what I can do. It's not always straightforward.' She checked her notes. 'You need to check in to Ward 2A at nine am a week on Thursday. I'll operate early on Friday morning, and with any luck you'll be out of here in under a week. OK?'

I went straight home. I was going to plan a whole festival around this event, parties before and after, culminating in the planting of my uterus. What a hoot. A hysterectomy hoe-down. A womb wake.

I got my friend Sandra to officiate. Thirteen women sat in a circle in my backyard. Sandra anointed the circle with rose water and lit a fire in a cast-iron pot in the middle. She had asked everyone to write what they wanted to give up on a slip of paper, and one by one we spoke, putting our papers into the fire. I was giving up my womb, others were giving up smoking or rotten lovers or self-flagellation or biting their fingernails. When we'd all said our bit, we played violins and cellos and guitars and flutes and danced and drank and sang all night.

A week later I woke up from surgery to find that Iraq had invaded Kuwait. A red-letter day all round. I was on a ward with four other women, all in their seventies. They taught me how to play Newmarket, and we gambled for pennies every morning after breakfast. They taught me lots of hilarious expressions, like 'He's so daft he couldn't get a fart out of a colander'. There was a lot of talk about farting; a nosy person is said to want to know 'how many farts make an ounce'. One stuffy nurse was 'about as handy as a pig with side pockets'. We laughed so hard I nearly burst my stitches more than once.

I went home to Joe and eleven-year-old Claire with my

Amazonian uterus in a brown paper bag. It turned out that I'd had a disease called adenomyosis – tumours filling the space between the inner and outer walls of the womb – so it was perfectly shaped, but huge. They'd cut it in half in their post-op routine autopsy, so I tied it together with a red silk ribbon and put it in the freezer until I'd be strong enough for the planting. Joe didn't want anything to do with it. He made it plain that he thought I was nuts. Claire was grossed out completely by the sight of her foetal home, though she did have a look. Others came especially to see it, all wrapped up like the gift of life. It's not often that we get a chance to eyeball what runs us.

The planting happened a month later, a more subdued and meditative affair. My friends bought me a medlar tree – the 'tight-assed fruit' – and we dug it into the ground with all our wishes. Two women who had been trying for a long time wished to conceive children, and both, as it happens, gave birth to girls the following year. I wished for courage and confidence. That's still on the way, I guess. But I haven't missed my womb at all, because I know just where it is.

With Claire gone, I knew I needed a boost. So I called Franny, and Franny called Sandra. I thought back to when I left home: no ceremony, no tears. Did Tildy ever miss me just a little bit? I doubt it. I think she was too busy missing herself.

I walked under a bald and humming moon to where my friends were waiting, crying all the way. But I knew, for tonight anyway, I'd be fine.

Gimme a Minute

Hello?

   Daddy, it's me.

   Susie?

   Susie.

   Ah.

   How are you feeling?

Daddy started to cry. Not out loud, but I could tell.

   Gimme a minute. I'll call you back.

   OK.

I placed the phone in its cradle and smoked one, two, then three cigarettes before the phone rang again. Daddy is probably doing the same thing, I thought.

Hi, Daddy. But it was Claire. I explained that I was waiting for a call and promised to phone her later. The phone didn't ring again.

A week later I got a card in the mail. It had brightly

coloured fishes swimming all over it. The postmark said Houston, and I recognized my daddy's handwriting, a spidery scrawl.

I'm sorry, it said. That's all.

I started packing.

Crazy

The twins have refused to speak to me since my face-off with our father. They prefer me crazy, and they're having none of it. Their world view remains unchanged. I guess it's easier that way. I never saw a lot of them anyhow, so it doesn't matter much. Not too much.

They did come to see me in England once. It was their first and only time outside the USA. They didn't like it here, and told me I was crazy to want to live in a country where the sun didn't shine. When I assured them that, indeed, it did, but this was February, they both just snorted. They couldn't wait to get home.

Frank and Fred spent their week with me playing solitaire. Tildy told me once that while she was carrying the twins she could hardly move, she was so huge, so she played solitaire for hours at a time. She had clubs and hearts and diamonds and spades in her dreams. I don't know if habits can be picked up *in utero*, but it sure seems like it. Brother and T'other are devoted to that game. I tried to show them around, take them to museums, galleries, the countryside, but they didn't want to go. They just sat at my kitchen table playing solitaire.

Claire was two then; she tried to engage them in some baby talk, but they didn't want to know. They found her annoying, and kept their cards in their pockets on the rare occasions when they weren't playing. They didn't trust her, was the feeling. They just didn't know anything about kids.

The truth is, I don't really know them, either. They are a tight unit, self-contained and wary of intruders into their country. I changed their diapers and washed their faces, and acted as an intermediary between them and the rest of the world when they were small. They seem to resent this now; I was an inadequate mother. I was only two myself then, and three and four and five. But still, it wasn't good enough, and they hate me for it, without even realizing that they do. That's the only way I can explain their unmitigated fury when they found out I'd been to talk to Daddy. They called me at Bubba's.

Goddamnit to hell, Susie, what do you think you are doin'? Will you just Goddamn grow up, for Christ sake?

I need to do this, guys. It doesn't have to affect you.

You know Daddy's sick. He's too old for this bullshit. You might kill him, did you ever think of that?

Yeah. I did.

It was an unsatisfactory conversation, which concluded with Frank and Fred washing their hands of me. I haven't talked to them since. This hurts my heart. But I'll get over it. I put it out of my mind. I put it out of my mind. I put it out of my mind. I put it out of my mind.

Going to the River

I walk to the river every day, half hoping to drown. The river is in me. It is a source of life, and I can save my people there. But there are risks.

Why doncha push off, ya daft twit! Go on! Push off! I heard him say as I approached. He was an old man, waving one arm around and talking to no one I could see. He was neatly dressed, trousers perfectly creased, spotless white shirt and beige windbreaker. He carried a large holdall that looked empty, or held only – what? A letter home? Sandwiches? House keys? A hacksaw?

As I passed him I caught his eye, then looked away quickly when he turned his wrath on me. I quickened my pace but he raised his voice. *Blimey, she's no chicken. Buk-buk-buk-buk-buk*, he clucked after me. *Buk-buk-buk-buk-buk*, gradually fading until the river took over with its slosh and glug. I wondered, who dressed that man? Who ironed his shirt and pants?

I've been to so many places, done so many things. What do I remember? The heat, the cold, blurred impressions of people and feelings and earth and air. What do I never forget? Claire. Daddy's hands. A swan king, majestic and stern, all his attention fixed on me.

I'm a grandmother now. Claire and Rob, her partner, live in Houston, while I stay on in this English town. Rob is an engineer for NASA. Claire met him the last summer we spent in my father's house, the summer before he died. It was a whirlwind romance. Rob flew back to England with us and they were married at Christmastime. How history repeats itself!

Hannah is just six months old. I was there for the birth, of course. I miss seeing her every day, but I know to keep some distance. She's not mine the way Claire was, and I don't trust myself around babies. They are so vulnerable.

I don't see many people these days. My neighbours occasionally, the local shopkeepers, Sandra when she's got a minute. Kevin, who you could call my boyfriend, I see about once a week. He'd like it to be more frequent than that, but I can't do it. I don't want anyone that close to me.

Sometimes, downtown, I run into kids I've taught, but I hardly go downtown any more. Everything I need is available in the local shops. I can hear my vowels changing more definitely as the years go by. Most days I feel as if I'm wearing a mask.

I am still regularly interrupted by events. I was watering my garden the other day when Pippa came from next door with her little watering can to help. She's two and a half. *I'll help,* she squeaked, *I have a can*. She followed me around the yard, getting refills from my hose. But her mother came to take her away.

Come on, you. Come and eat your tea, Kerry said, hoisting the child up into her arms. She smiled briefly at me, then turned and went. Shame swept over me in a hot red rush. I felt my heart clench.

She knows, I thought. *They all know*. These feelings make me hang my head. I know they're irrational, and that people have got better things to do than cluck at me, but there you are. There I am. It's not that I'm not happy, it's just that happy to me isn't happy to most people.

Daddy died three years ago. He was eighty-one, just went to bed one night and didn't wake up. I wasn't responsible.

Clearing out the house was weird. The last time Bubba and the twins and I were all together was at Tildy's funeral, and a lot has changed since then. Houston was still hot and close, but Frank and Fred were cold and distant, just wanted to get it over with, sell or junk the lot. Bubba felt pretty much the same. I wanted to take time, to look carefully through each drawer and closet, to find something I knew must be there. The twins finally flew home to Greensboro in disgust. *Just send the money when you're done. We're outa here*.

Bubba and I were going through an old filing cabinet when we came across several letters from Presidents, medals and commendations. We were amazed! Daddy had kept all this quiet. He was much more highly decorated than we knew. A humble man. In among the records of his bravery we found a card, a Father's Day card, from me. The year wasn't written, but I must have been seven or eight years old. I wrote, 'To the

best daddy from your little sweetieheart. xxxooo. Love, Susie.'
It was the only such item we found. Everything else was business.

All the years add up to this: we never really know each other at all, not at all. And trying just makes the gulf wider and more obvious. But we have to try. Don't we?

My trip to my father's conscience was eventful, and not. He owned up, apologized, wept and spluttered. He blamed the drink. He hung his head. I went home to England, relieved but somehow hollowed out. *What now?* I thought. *What's next? Am I better now?* And the answer is, yes, some days. And I'm pretty sure the cycle has stopped with me. I'm assuming a cycle, of course. I'll never be sure about that. But a cycle is comforting.

I recently had my palm read. Took a trip to the seaside, just for a change of scenery. Sometimes the river gets me down. Gypsy Rose, she was called. She looked like a matron lady, no shawls or bangles, just Marks and Spencer, and a hairdo like Margaret Thatcher's. I sat down on a wobbly wooden chair in her tiny room. She held and stroked my hand, but looked at my face. After a minute she started tsk-tsk-ing. *Poor thing*, she cooed, *you've had it tough. Am I right?* I felt tears spring up from nowhere and blinked them back. I nodded. *But it's over now. It won't happen again.* But it will, I thought. It happens again and again. It plays like *Star Trek* re-runs, always on some channel or other, crackling away at the back of my mind.

Any good news? I heard myself ask. Gypsy Rose studied my palm this time, then looked at me and smiled. *I see a tall dark stranger.* She dropped my hand and folded hers together.

That'll be five pounds, unless you want the crystal ball and Tarot, which will make it ten.

I paid her and walked down to the beach. The water sparkled in the sunlight, and I took off my sandals and waded in. Water has always been my element.

The Mountain

There was a mountain – not a mountain really, just a big hill – right behind our house in Riverside. It was called, pretentiously I guess, considering its size, Mount Rubidoux. It was red dirt, rock and pines, and a kind of haven for me when we lived there. Red ants and rattlesnakes all over the place, but I'd run straight up the side of that mountain barefooted and feel safer than I've ever felt anywhere in the world. I'd spend hours making trails with Indian markers, or building wikkiups and hogans in the cool spaces underneath the cedars, where there was protection from the sun steaming off the stones.

One day I was there with my friend Katy. It was particularly hot and we were deep in under the trees, lying on our backs on the dense layer of pine needles that I liked better than my bed, only partly because it smelled so nice. Katy asked me this: *What's the best feeling you've ever had?* Well, that took some thinking. I considered eating ice cream on a hot, hot day, and winning all the running races at school, and getting As on my report card. I was about to settle on swimming – my fish-feelings always kept me under water for longer than anyone thought possible and I believed I *was* water, not just in it – when Katy said, *I'll tell you my best feeling if you shut your eyes.* So I settled back to listen and this is what she told me: *Finger in the flame for as long as I can hold it there. Finger in the flame, finger in the flame, finger in the flame.* Her breathing had become heavier and faster, then she sighed. I opened my eyes and she was looking at me with her right index finger held up between us. I saw a redness there I hadn't noticed before. I must have looked shocked, because she laughed and nudged my side. *Race you to the big rock*, she said, and stood up running. I followed.

She beat me to the big rock; she was a year older and six inches taller than me. A lizard scrambled across it and out of sight as we climbed up the side. It was high noon, a heat-stung stillness in the air. We sat in silence for a while. I was reconsidering my choice when something came to me. It was the time when Uncle Bug came to visit us in Whittier. He was a Forest Ranger, living then in Arizona, high in the mountains. He was the object of most serious devotion and awe to us kids – probably because he saw us seldom enough to genuinely like it when he did – though for some reason Mama never cared much for him; something to do with the ladies' lingerie that always littered his room on the rare occasions we went to see him. Or just that he was Daddy's kin, not hers. On this visit he was helping us make a cake, or showing us how, and when he got to the eggbeater part he said sternly, *Now you kids keep your fingers away from the beater, OK? You could get hurt.* From that point on I couldn't take my eyes off those spinning blades, propelled as they were by Uncle Bug's fine energy. I was entranced, and before anyone, including me, could stop it, I'd stuck my fingers straight into the middle of the thing. We all gaped at the blood pouring into the batter, and then my uncle got his wits back and wrapped my hand in a dish towel. *What'd you do that for?* he asked, perplexed. *I had to.* That was all I could say.

I told Katy my choice, and I could tell she approved. We were getting hot on the big rock so we headed for cover, under a stand of cedars nearby. The red earth under my body, the moving, enveloping heat in the fragrant shade on the side of a hill; this would be my choice now. Well, one of them. Probably couldn't choose at all, really. Marrying Joe might come close, but then look where that got me in the end. Maybe I was seeking the burn, the blood, without realizing it. Maybe I got what I wanted.

Sometimes I think I left my girl there, that if I went back I'd find her there still, darting through the undergrowth, loose and alert and swift and safe. Held briefly but well by a mountain.

Acknowledgements

I want to thank the following for their help:

My readers and seeders, as I like to think of them: Judith Catan, Brenda Cullen, Sandra Dartnell, Jude Grundy, Peter Haywood, Greg Harrison, Jeff Horne, Jon Horne, Andy Lebrecht, Rita Perrin, Hannah Twist, Bob Welch, Kate Welch, Nicky Welch-Jasnoch, and James Whitford.

My necessary and impeccable writers group: Kate Coffey, Gerry Curran, David Harmer, Lesley Marshall, Joi Rathbone, Jim Sheard, and John Turner.

Lesley Glaister for her wonderful teaching and support. Katie Owen for her encouragement. My brilliant agent John Saddler. Antonia Hodgson, my editor at Virago. All involved in the MA/Writing course at Sheffield Hallam University.

Ma & Pa, for rich soil to grow in.

And Jenny Frances, who opened my dream door.

TEMPTING FAITH DiNAPOLI

Lisa Gabriele

Sweet, sarcastic, completely exasperating Faith DiNapoli is determined to mend her family's dysfunctional ways. Not easy with the DiNapolis, already run out of town once and constantly teetering on the edge of disrepute. Even harder as Faith has a tendency to misread everything – including the Bible and her mother's diary . . .

And despite her dreams of respectability, Faith is struggling with her own temptations: dope, drink, boys and short, short skirts. Will she end up like her hard-working, tough-talking, fabulous mother, abandoned with four kids before she's thirty? What chance does she have, attending a school her mother has nicknamed 'The Slut Daycare Centre'?

'Fresh and honest, funny and sad'
Beverly Donofrio, author of *Riding in Cars with Boys*

'A lively, fast-moving debut which, for all its humour, is also a memorable story of a single mother's fight for survival'
Irish Examiner

'Beautifully observed . . . hard to put down' *New Books*

RIDING IN CARS WITH BOYS

Beverly Donofrio

Beverly Ann Donofrio didn't start out bad, although it didn't help that her initials spelled the word out in bold across her school folder. But when she learns there's no money to send her to college, Bev loses interest in everything but riding around in cars, drinking, smoking and rebelling against authority. She's looking for trouble, and she gets it. 'Trouble' as in, 'Is she in trouble?' As in pregnant. After her teenage marriage fails, she's left to bring up her baby alone. But Bev is too smart, too funny and too determined to live life to the full to give up.

A terrifically honest and touching memoir, *Riding in Cars with Boys* is a story of a teenage mother who, as her son grows up, becomes an adult herself.

'Every swoop and dive of this roller-coaster life presents another off-kilter view of humanity. Makes you realise that even very, very B-A-D girls can redeem themselves with pluck, luck, and humour'
Jacki Lyden, author of *Daughter of the Queen of Sheba*

'She lives and writes as though she was born without brakes – it's shrewd, touching, funny and astonishing'
Joanna Lumley

'A wonderful book! Her story has all the bad girl freshness and vitality to make it true to the bone'
Susan Minot

Now you can order superb titles directly from Virago